THE PROPHECY

MONIQUE SINGLETON

VINCI
BOOKS

Writing is a beautiful way to express yourself.
I understand this now.
With every book I write I find even more to write about.
This is my tenth book. The second in the Prophecy series and definitely not the last.
My fantasy is just starting to unfold.
But writing is just writing, without readers.
Readers make it a story worth telling.
All thanks go to you, my readers, my muses.

Vinci Books

vinci-books.com

Published by Vinci Books Ltd in 2026

1

Copyright © Monique Singleton 2020

The EU GPSR authorised representative is Logos Europe, 9 rue Nicolas
Poussion, 17000 La Rochelle, France
contact@logoseurope.eu

By Monique Singleton

The Prophecy Series

Assassin's Choice
The Prophecy
Final Stand

The Dominion Series

The Devil You Know
I AM the Storm
To Hell and Back
Insurrection

The Primal Series

Primal Nature
Nature of the Beast
The Beast Inside
Into the Lion's Den
Knife's Edge

Prologue

Life seemed so straightforward a few months ago.

Kill two targets and get out.

Then return to my real reason for living; find out who's responsible for my mother's death. I wanted to terminate him—or her—in a very painful, prolonged and terrible manner.

Whether I lived or died after achieving my revenge was completely irrelevant to me.

And now?

Now, I'm the centre of what is turning out to be a world changing prophecy.

How the fuck did that happen?

And another thing; I'm involved in not one but two romances. And to make things worse, both of my lovers have a legitimate claim to me as their soulmate.

The ideal solution seemed to be a threesome. It could work you know. If they weren't so different. And both so very, very possessive. Oh yeah, small detail. One is of the feline persuasion; a Sabre-tooth, and the other is a Werewolf.

Cat versus dog. The age-old adversity.

Times about a thousand.

It's a wonder I'm still sane.

That I am is solely the accomplishment of one man: Ash. The Blackfoot Shaman.

If he is a man that is.

He could be anything.

…Probably is.

Chapter One

No one said it would be easy, but this is ridiculous.

My two beaus act like prepubescent adolescents.

Both of them.

Add the whole cat and dog thing to the equation and you get an idea why I'm going crazy.

"Why choose?" That's what Ash said. Yeah, why choose?

Well, I have more than enough reasons now why I should have chosen.

They have to share me. We established that months ago. Neither of them was particularly enthusiastic about the idea, but you'd think that they could at least be civil about it all. Pretend to be adults.

Metisse is the worst.

He's a lot younger than Gabriel, but I expected more from him because of his worldly and privileged upbringing. He was brought up in a society where strong females are the norm. His mother was—and really still is—the leader of one of the most influential Sabre clans in the world. He should know better.

Gabriel started off okay, but his patience with his rival was short to start with, and Metisse's childish behaviour pushed him to return in kind. Now he's just as bad.

Single life never looked as attractive as it does now. This was definitely not what I envisioned my life to become.

Four months ago, I was alone and my only goal in life was revenge for my mother's death. Romance was the last thing on my mind.

Ever since my mother was taken from me by the Council, my only drive has been to find the miscreants responsible for her death.

I knew she was dead.

There wasn't a body, but there was so much blood she could never have survived. The bastards didn't even leave me her corpse to grieve.

I was alone. Twelve years old and on the run from a mighty organisation that wanted me dead. I had no idea why, only that it was because of who I was. What I was.

I'm half Sabre and half Werewolf. A hybrid. The only one apparently.

My mother was the queen of a Sabre clan, my father the alpha of a Werewolf pack; traditionally sworn enemies.

Against all odds, they fell in love. Then they had me and all hell broke loose. The Council wanted me because of an old prophecy. I am apparently the Lamaq; a woman of two worlds, destined to overthrow their tyranny. Cantix and his sidekick Aquanaris would be out of a job, and hopefully minus their heads.

They ruled the paranormal world together. Not officially, no, that was the Council. But the members of the so-called ruling committee couldn't even fart without approval from Cantix.

The seer—Aquanaris—was feared throughout the entire world. She could see what others tried to hide. Saw rebellion before it even started.

Except with me.

She never saw through my disguise. Never knew the one person they hunted most was in their inner circle, closing in on them with every assassination they tasked me to perform. Cantix trusted me and I suspect he enjoyed my bad-ass petulant ways. I suppose I amused him.

I don't think Aquanaris ever completely fell for it, not really. She knew there was something about me. I would have loved to see their faces when they heard the news; their top assassin was the Lamaq. The chosen one. The woman from the prophecy. The one they hunted.

And now, here I was, trying to gather an army to combat the Council. I have to convince people—who hate each other with a vengeance—to work together against their real enemy. They have to put their petty differences aside and go for the real deal.

Sounds easy, right?

Walk in the park.

Wrong.

I was way out of my depth here. Up shit creek without a boat, never mind a paddle.

Thank goodness for Ash.

Ash—or Askuwheteau, if you want a tongue twister—is the Shaman of the Blackfoot tribe, he is also the unofficial leader of the Wolves, though he will always contradict that. He's been around for God knows how long. Hundreds, maybe thousands of years. I don't even know what he is exactly. He's not a Werewolf, but he is revered amongst them.

He's an enigma.

And he's my best friend.

Ash helped me find my way in the life-changing madness I found myself in. Convince me there was structure to this, reason. Well, I can't find it. So, I just took his word for it.

He grounded me.

Not that he told me things outright. Oh no. He helped me find out for myself. He guided me without pushing me in a direction. He stood beside me.

My big friend was—and is—my rock.

In a different way than my two beaus, thank God for that. Another one would have been way too many. No, he actually helped me find my way and supported me.

Literally sometimes.

And then there's Charmaine. The de-facto leader of the Sabres. I know, Metisse was the official leader, but even he referred to his mother. She's the anchor of the clan. She's the most natural chieftain I have ever seen.

Charmaine's my mother-in-law, Metisse's mother, but she's also my confidant. My mentor even. She's such a strong woman; I look up to her no end.

There was one very unsettling thing about her though. She knew my mother. And every now and then I felt she knew so much more than she was telling me. About the prophecy, my family and mostly; about me.

My beau's.

Metisse the haughty arrogant Sabre, rich and powerful. And Gabriel, his complete antithesis. A biker. A Werewolf. Poor in monetary terms, but rich in family and the loyalty of his pack.

They're each other's opposites. Rich versus poor. Status versus outcast. Cat versus dog.

They had to share me. I recognised them both as my soulmates. They were bonded to me and I to them. This strange love triangle's an anomaly. Wolves and Sabres don't mingle. They hate each other. Always have. But here they had to live together. Quite the challenge.

There were benefits—mostly for me—but it wasn't smooth sailing. As I said earlier; they drove me mad. Both acted like spoiled teenagers.

I didn't have time for all this crap.

Not then, now, not ever.

We were all pawns in the game destiny played with us; the prophecy. Seems that a woman of two worlds—me—would overthrow the Council.

The prophecy very conveniently didn't explain how I was supposed to do that monumental feat.

I'm not a strategist. I'm an assassin. A loner. I had no idea how to dethrone the Council.

But I did know I wanted to.

I had to.

For my parents.

...For me.

Okay, you're up to speed.

If you now think that this is all too ridiculous to be true.

...welcome to my world.

Chapter Two

'I'm not a leader.'

I tried to make the statement as compelling and clear as possible. I knew I wasn't and never would be leader material. It was time the rest acknowledged that as well.

Yeah. Right.

Like that was going to happen. They all looked to me for guidance. Me!

'You are now.' Ash answered with a big smile. Sometimes, just sometimes, I wanted to knock that smile off his face. Good thing I couldn't reach it. The big man loved to bait me. And I presumed he was doing just that.

'Seriously, Trish,' he continued. All earnest again. 'You are the chosen one. The one person everyone refers to. You must lead us.'

"Chosen One." God, how I hated that phrase.

'How the hell am I supposed to do that?' I paced the room. I didn't want this, but no one was asking.

'I don't know how the fuck to lead people in battle. I'm an assassin, for fuck's sake. I'm not good with groups.'

There were a lot of "fucks" in my vocabulary as of late. What, with this crap and my two lovers at each other's throats all the time, it's inevitable.

'I work alone.'

'Not any more you don't.' There was no hesitation. No emotion. He was clearly stating the obvious. All the people who joined us in the past month were here because of me. Me, and a stupid prophecy they all wanted to believe in.

Yeah, well. I still want to believe in Father Christmas. Doesn't mean he's real. Wanting is not enough.

'Ash.' I tried a different tactic. 'I don't know what to do. I'm not leader material. I don't know how to motivate people, how to get them to fight for me, for a cause. That's not me. I'll get everyone killed.'

Nope, didn't work either. He just sat there and watched me get it out of my system. The man had patience. I didn't. Probably never will.

I stood still and ran my hand through my long red hair. I wanted to pull it out. Scream. Anything that would let out the tension that ate at me.

It wouldn't help. I knew that. Somewhere deep down inside a voice kept repeating this was my life now. I was here for a reason. They followed me for a reason.

Yeah, well, fucked if I knew what it was.

I sighed, squeezed my brow with my hand and closed my eyes. Let it all go away, please.

Nope, still there when I opened them. Only now Ash stood in front of me and looked down at my pathetic excuse for leadership.

He took my hands in his, dwarfing them. I felt like a small child every time he did that. He was so big, and I felt so tiny. Small, but safe.

'You need to have more faith in yourself, Trish.' He

made it all sound so easy. Okay, I'll do that. Sure. That simple, huh?

I swear the man could read my mind, he started to laugh. I looked up from under my eyebrows and bit my lip. My feline claws descended a bit and almost punctured the skin of his hands. He stayed put, the smile still plastered to his lips. I relaxed. The claws became regular nails again and I returned the smile.

'I suppose you find that funny?' I asked in mock anger.

He nodded. 'And so should you. Trish, there is no escaping who you are, or what you are. You might just as well embrace it. It will make life a lot easier for you.'

'And for me,' I heard from behind me. I let go of Ash's hands and turned to face an equally grinning Gabriel. I hadn't even heard him slink into the room. He liked to do that; surprise me.

'Is life with me that bad?' I asked him surprised.

'You have no idea.' The smile on his face was ear to ear. I tried to look angry but lost the fight quickly. I looked to Ash for support, he just shrugged and backed away laughing.

'Oh no, I'm not intervening in this one.'

'Wimp.' I muttered under my breath, just loud enough for him to hear.

'Oh, so your life is hard, is it?' I advanced on my lover who put his hands up in mock fear as he took a step back. At the last moment he reached out and took me in a massive bear hug, laughing all the time.

'You have no idea,' he repeated.

I tickled him. My fingers deep in his left side, just under the ribs. He's extremely ticklish and I know exactly the right spots. He doubled up, trying in vain to escape my hands. No way; when I have a hold, I don't let go.

Oh no. He changed tactics and went on the offence, finding my ticklish parts. Now I had to defend myself from someone who was a lot taller and heavier than me. Gabriel was spurred on by my struggles and Ash's laughter. It was silly. Childish, but we all needed this.

Suddenly Gabe stopped and stood up straight. Confused, I looked up at his face and then turned to follow his gaze. Metisse stood in the doorway, his face red and flushed; with jealousy probably. He hated to see me with Gabriel. It sparked off many arguments Between my beau's, and also between Metisse and myself.

Gabriel let go of me, his hands dropped to his sides as he watched what his love-opponent would do next.

I could see the struggle in Metisse's body language. He was tense, his clenched fists stiff by his sides. His thin lips were pulled into a straight line, echoing the anger I saw in his bright ochre eyes.

What would he do? Turn and leave? It wouldn't be the first time. He had a habit of avoiding situations like this. There would be days when I wouldn't see him at all. Other times he would be protectively, almost territorially present. He wouldn't leave my side. It was one extreme or the other. Absent or oppressively close.

He made up his mind and walked stiffly over to me where he stopped much too close. I felt Gabriel stand his ground. He didn't step back. Again, the ochre eyes flared as Metisse glared at Gabe over my head.

Okay, this was starting to piss me off again. Any good feelings I had were replaced by irritation. Thanks, Metisse. I thought.

He kissed me on the lips, making a point. Yeah, to Gabe, not to me. God, these two were getting on my nerves with their petty macho bullshit. They both stood so close to me I felt boxed in.

I had no time for this crap. With a shrug I sidestepped away from both of them. If they wanted to pose, then they could do it without me. Fuck that.

I heard murmurs behind me, they were at it again, shooting insults at each other. Did they honestly think I didn't hear them? I'm not deaf, you know.

I turned around, mad as hell. 'Can it.' The tone of my voice was hard enough to stop them mid-sentence. 'Grow up, both of you.'

They each looked at me with surprised faces and a "he started it" on the tip of their tongue. 'Don't,' I warned them. I must have looked serious, because they both shut up and looked embarrassed, as well they should. They were acting like children arguing over a toy. I'm not a toy and I will not accept this kind of behaviour.

Okay, I know this threesome was my idea. But if they didn't agree, then they should have said so.

It's not really that simple, I know.

They are both bound to me. They can't really refuse.

Not without endangering their own existence.

Chapter Three

The woman of two worlds.

That's who I'm supposed to be. I guess it's true in as much as I'm a hybrid. I'm half in the Sabre world and half in the Wolves'.

Quite the paradox.

Not just a cat and dog shifter thing. There are more differences between the two worlds. The Sabres are sophisticated, educated, rich mostly, at least the ones here.

The Wolves are exactly the opposite. They scrape their existence together on a daily basis. Quite often gaining an income from less than legal opportunities.

They are however: direct, warm and honest among themselves and to me. I knew exactly where I was with the Wolves. Not so much with the Sabres.

Sabres are more political animals. Political, as in backstabbing.

My earlier run in with Mariah—the second-in-command in the clan—caused bad blood. The fact I officially bonded with Metisse hadn't helped either. She held a grudge. In the typical Sabre stubborn, short-sighted way. What was it with them? They lead a privileged life. They should be open minded.

Anyway, that's probably not fair of me.

This prophecy is seriously pissing me off.

I didn't ask for it, but I can't run away from it. It's part of me, I guess. It feels like a leach attached to my back I just can't seem to get rid of.

'Ash.' I walked up to the big man. Strode up would probably describe it better. The stubbornness in my nature refused to allow me to accept my destiny. I fought against it on a daily basis. I hated that everyone looked to me to decide what we would do. How the hell was I supposed to know? I'm not a general.

I'm an assassin.

By definition my kind doesn't form connections with others. We're loners. We rely solely on our own wits. We don't need anyone else and don't work well with others. And now I'm supposed to lead a rag-tag army against the most powerful force in the world.

No pressure, right?

Ash turned to face me, the big smile on his face was the customary way he greeted me.

It took the edge off my rage. I looked up at his beautiful colourful eyes and, as always, they calmed me even more. The soft movements of the swirling colours in his irises hypnotised me; placated me even.

I don't think it was a conscious thing he did, though you never knew with Ash. There was little he did without meaning. When I observed him looking at others the colours of his eyes varied; almost as though they adapted to how he viewed people and to the bond he did—or didn't—have with them.

It warmed me. I loved being around the Shaman. He was a true friend, more than that, he was my mentor. I counted on him to help me find my way. Not that he gave me direct answers. Nooooo, that would be too easy. He pointed me in a direction. Asked counter questions to every query I posed. He made me think. And occasionally, he would just tell me how things were.

'Trish.' His deep warm voice sent chills down my spine. Not in a lustful way, our relationship wasn't like that. Oh sure, I've wondered. But it's not like that. Besides, I have my hands full with my two lovers as it is. Unless of course I could swap the two of them for Ash. Hmmm. That's a thought.

I looked up again and blushed at the big smile on his face. Was he reading my mind? He said he couldn't, but I'm not so sure. He chuckled, further strengthening my suspicion he knew exactly what I was thinking about.

'How can I help you?' he changed the subject we both hadn't voiced out loud.

I swallowed and concentrated on why I was here.

'I need to know more about the prophecy.'

'What exactly do you need to know?' There he was again, answering me with another question.

'What can you tell me?' Two can play that game. I smiled. He chuckled.

Ash indicated the two chairs and we sat down. As usual, I sank deep into the cushions, again feeling very small and insignificant.

'How old is the prophecy?' I asked. Ash would know.

'Very old,' he answered. Right, that helped, thanks Ash.

I huffed and bit my lip which caused him to laugh again at my implied sarcasm. 'Almost five centuries old.'

Okay, now we were getting somewhere. I cocked my head and shrugged my shoulders in an attempt to convince him to continue. The question-and-reluctant-answer technique would keep us here all day.

'There was a shaman; a woman. Quite revolutionary for those days,' he continued. 'Kimi was in tune to nature all around her. The paranormal was strong in her. There was relative peace then, the humans and paranormals lived together in harmony. The tribes all had their own territories and skirmishes were few. That changed when one fraction of the paranormal society aspired to take over the territory of the Blackfoot tribe.'

'The hunting and fishing in that area was optimal, there were mountains and big expansions of grass where the buffalo roamed. It was prime territory. The tribe was strong and healthy. They were prosperous. All of this was a thorn in they eye of the shaman of a neighbouring tribe; the Cree.'

'Matunaagd, their chieftain, was a paranormal like Kimi. His name was pertinent; "he who fights". He was a violent man, forever jealous of his neighbours' possessions. He never understood their assets were the result of the balance they created with their surroundings. He just saw what they had, and he didn't.'

I closed my eyes and settled down to a good—and most likely long—story. Ash was the best storyteller I had ever known, he was able to transport the listener directly into the scenes in the tale.

'The Siksika Blackfoot have always been a peaceful tribe, but also quite competitive. They "fought" their wars with other fractions of their nation and their neighbours in battles that rarely ended in death or bloodshed. They counted coup instead. There was an understanding between the tribes. The Siksika were the strongest—they achieved the most coups—but were lenient and friendly with their competitors. This way of doing battle was acknowledged by all tribes in the neighbourhood of their territory. All except the Cree tribe led by Matunaagd.'

Ash's voice took on a darker tone and the pictures I saw I'm my mind did the same.

'The altercations between the two nations started in the customary manner with a lot of posturing, stealing of each other's dogs and counting coups. Then Matunaagd changed the face of war. He led his tribe in the slaughter of the Blackfoot warriors.'

'He didn't stop there, he turned towards the tipis housing the women and children and massacred many of them.'

Ash's voice was hollow with the memory.

'Kimi thrust herself before the women and children who fled the scene in panic. She managed to hold off the Cree until most escaped, using her paranormal powers that greatly out-performed those of Matunaagd.'

'She joined the refugees and they went to their brother Kainai Blackfoot tribe. There they watched in bewilderment as Matunaagd raped their home territory. His tribe hunted the bison till there were hardly any left, they warred with neighbours, killed crops and animals, and scorched the earth.'

I felt the pain of the Blackfoot tribe as they watched everything they loved disappear before their eyes. Everything they'd accomplished in the many centuries of dedication. All because of a greedy man with a massive ego. The similarities with Cantix, and many human leaders for that matter, were astounding.

Would people never learn? I guess not.

'Matunaagd watched his neighbours with an eagle eye, always coveting what they owned.' Ash's voice resonated. 'His reign of terror expanded through the plains and into what is now Canada. His toxic reach became more extensive all the time. As a paranormal he lived for centuries. All the way up till the Europeans discovered America. With them he discovered a people who were not only far distanced from paranormal talents, their religions outlawed them. Now the tables were turned; he and his tribe were persecuted by the fanatical Christian colonisers. They were hunted and decimated.'

'Kimi thought to find an ally with the Europeans, but was greatly disappointed. They didn't distinguish between tribes, but persecuted all as the same. The Blackfoot were murdered along with their enemies. No one was spared.'

'Kimi understood the new rulers of the land were even worse than Matunaagd had been. These white-faced strangers had no respect for nature, tradition or the spiritual world. Their priests were adamant; kill the heretics. Stamp out the devil worshippers; the paranormal.' Ash's voice was full of the pain he felt.

'They were persecuted without end.'

We were silent. It all sounded much too familiar. Anything different has always been hunted down by humans. They can't deal with diversity. People have to follow pre-set and narrow boundaries and anything that even dares to look outside of those constraints is crushed immediately.

'Kimi and her pack were wiped out by the new comers.' Ash's solemn tone pushed the pain deep inside. 'Few escaped,' he continued. 'One of them was Kimi's daughter; Hurit. She took on her mother's duties and became the new Shaman. The Prophecy was the legacy she received from her dying mother. Hurit passed it on through the ages.'

I urged him onwards. This was what I needed to know.

'The prophecy speaks of a woman of two worlds who will bring balance and peace.'

Yeah, I knew that part. 'Does it say which worlds?'

He shook his head. 'Prophecies are by definition vague and open for multiple interpretations. They are used and misused, according to the times, circumstances and vested interests.'

I nodded. This was not going well. Things were becoming even more complicated. If that were possible.

Ash continued his explanation. 'In times of great need the woman will gather the nations together to confront the oppressors. They will triumph. Not because of violence, but because of love.'

'Love?' That was a new part for me.

'Yes.'

That sounded so stupid. How could love win a war? Free a nation? Or in our case, smash the Council? Don't take me wrong, I wish it could. It was just that under the circumstances it all seemed very naive. The factions of the paranormal world were at each other's throats and then love is supposed to save us?

'Is that it?' I asked. Hopeful it wasn't and that he could explain more.

Instead he nodded. Shit.

'So what am I supposed to do with that?' I asked; dejected and quite annoyed.

Ash chuckled like you normally would at an irate child. Sometimes—just sometimes—I wanted to really wipe the smirk off his face. He must have known because he added to his explanation.

'There have been many readings of the Prophecy after Kimi and Hurit,' he continued. 'Oppression brought hope it would be applicable to many causes. None however, fulfilled the woman of two worlds concept. Not until now.' No pressure, huh.

'Why now? Why me?'

'Well, because you are of two worlds, in more than one way. Your parents are from different species. Different backgrounds. But also your life has turned from working with, to fighting against the Council.'

'I was never with the Council.'

'No, but that was only known by you. To the outside world, you have seen both sides.'

Okay, I'd give him that.

'And...'

My interest peaked. 'And what?'

'You are making Aquanaris very nervous. That is enough proof in itself.'

'Ash, how can so much rest on so little?' I asked after a few minutes silence. 'The prophecy seems so vague and open for so many interpretations. It can fit anything, and anyone. So what value does it have?'

He listened intently to my doubts.

'I can't understand why so many people want to believe in something so fickle. They give up their whole lives for what? For a few mumbled words of a dying woman?'

'They follow you not because the prophecy says so, and not because they are sure you are destined to save the world. They know the fragility of the words. They understand that nothing is definite.'

'Then why?'

'Because you give them hope. You dare to challenge the Council, the darkness. You look further than the boundaries Cantix has imposed on our kind. You defy his totalitarian regime. They see a warrior standing tall against oppression.'

'But I didn't start this to save the paranormal world,' I cried. 'All I wanted was revenge for my mother's death.'

'It doesn't matter to them why you stood up. It matters that you did. And then the prophecy falls into place.' He took my hands in his. 'Don't underestimate yourself Trish. You are a force to be reckoned with. You can pull this off. You will. Together, we will.'

I sighed. 'You hope.'

'No.' He lifted my chin up so that I looked him in the eye. 'I know.'

I tried to smile, but it didn't quite land.

'And, don't underestimate the powers of the Shamans. Kimi was very powerful. Who is to say she didn't force the future and your part in it?'

'Yeah, thanks,' I answered. 'No pressure.'

The big man laughed, kissed the top of my head and went back to his screen.

I would have to go with the flow.

God knows where it would all lead to.

Chapter Four

'How long have you been around?' It was a question that had continuously occupied my mind for the past months, ever since I met him.

Although I trusted him explicitly, Ash was still an anomaly for me. He looked up from his screen and smiled. He never got tired of my questions; the man had the patience of an angel. Come to think of it, maybe he was an angel. A tall, tattooed, kind of strange angel with a neon mohawk. But hey, who am I to judge? I'm the only hybrid ever known to man and paranormal alike.

If he was an angel, I'd have to change my whole outlook on creation, religion—I don't have one— and life in general. I was starting to hope he wasn't.

'Hundreds of years.'

'Hundreds or thousands?'

He sat back in his chair and observed me in that slightly patronising way that always riles me. 'Thousands.'

I pushed my irritation down. He was humouring me, so

what was I agitated about? To him I must sound like a curious child, always asking questions.

'What are you?' I decided on the direct approach.

'What am I?' That elicited a chuckle. It opened his face up and I had to smile.

I nodded.

Ash stood up and walked back to the couch where I sat. The chair opposite me groaned as he placed his awesome bulk in the soft cushions. 'For that I must go back to the beginning. Way back.' I nodded again. I loved it when he told me about the legends. They came alive with his words.

'When this world was formed, it was chaos. That was a time of magic. Of endless possibilities. Mankind used his and her full potential. Their minds were fully developed and they could use them to shape the world. It was a wonderful place. Until...' He loved cliffhangers. And as expected I took the bait.

'Until what?'

'Until mankind grew greedy. They wanted more.' He leaned forward giving emphasis to his words.

'Nothing was enough. Man wanted to rule the world. Use and abuse it to suit their whims. This did not go down with the the Almighty. She was displeased. She took their powers, and shut down a large portion of their minds. That way she made sure they could never reach their potential again. Mankind went back to the dark ages. Back to the Stone Age actually. They became dependant on nature again and were no longer the prime creation. Just one of many.'

His eyes bore into mine, the intensity gave me goosebumps.

'They lost the use of the majority of their brain. They lost their magic.'

Wow, that was unexpected. So mankind had at one point in time been able to use their complete brain. Ash sat back again in the chair and smiled benevolently.

'In some, a glint of what once was, was resurrected. Those were the Chosen Ones. They possessed a shadow of the talents of old, but they were looked upon with suspicion. They were different and could do strange things: shift, magic, read minds. They were a threat to those who were ignorant. The talented were hunted, murdered, and burned along with Nature's creatures.'

'So the Almighty created guardians. Those who would watch over the creations, both gifted and not. The guardians would preserve the old gifts and protect the innocent. They were called Elementals.'

'You're an Elemental?' It wasn't really a question anymore. It all fell into place. Who he was. What he was.

'Yes.'

'I have been around for many centuries. I travelled with the first settlers over the land bridge to the American continent. These were a spiritually advanced people who became the Native Americans. They were—and are—in tune with the magic in the world.'

'That's why they welcomed the Wolves.'

'Yes. The Wolves and any other paranormal creatures. They hold the key to the peace between the gifted and the non-gifted.'

'What do you do? I mean, as an Elemental? What is your mission in life.'

'I protect the gifted from the mortals and the mortals from the gifted.' Ash was nothing if not cryptic.

Chapter Five

Ash was a true hive of information when it came to other Wolf packs. He must know just about every pack in the US, and some further afar than that.

Gabriel, his pack and I, gladly picked Ash's brain for the location of the packs and the names of the alphas. It turned out that there were Werewolves in almost all heavily forested areas in the US plus in most of the big cities. I found that last piece of information astounding.

'In the cities?' I asked Ash. He nodded. 'But wouldn't that make it hard to hunt? And what do they prey on?'

'Some have degenerated to the expectations humans have and prey on the homeless.' There was sorrow in his voice. 'They have lost their way. Others are more fortunate and have prospered, which allows them to hunt out of town. But the majority of the packs live off whatever meat they can get. That often involves working in the meat markets and slaughterhouses. They are suited to that work and have less qualms than mortals.'

'Yeah, I can see that.' A thought occurred to me; 'how

do they camouflage their immortality?' It would be difficult to hide in a society as keyed to age and longevity as the humans.

'Most don't stay in one city for more than one or two years. They are basically drifters, nomads.'

'Bikers?'

'Yes, often. The biker lifestyle suits them very well. People avoid bikers, and the hierarchy of a Wolf pack greatly resembles that of a hard-core biker club.'

'And it helps to get around.' Gabriel added. 'We're inconspicuous as bikers. No one wants to have anything to do with us. Anyone who does, is easily scared off. Even the cops leave us alone. Well, anyone but you.' He laughed as he joined us.

'Yeah and aren't you glad I'm not quickly impressed?'

'Definitely.' He kissed me on the forehead.

'You have quite the reputation.' I continued.

'We do. Most of it's bullshit, some isn't. Here in Weisland we're avoided as outlaws and also as Native Americans. That stigma rubs off on us and aids to our chosen isolation. You know the Native Americans fall under reservation law, right?' I nodded. 'The cops leave the policing to the elders. They in turn know who and what we are.'

Ash continued: 'This is a structure you see in many of the packs. They hide in plain sight.'

'But you know how to find them.'

'I travelled. A long time ago I made it my goal to find the packs. Most of them are descended directly from the First Three, though not all. There were more Wolves who came after them.'

'How long did you travel?'

'About a hundred years.'

'Wasn't that difficult? I mean you do kind of stand out in a crowd.'

'Yes, I do. So for a while I joined a travelling circus. That allowed me to be out in the open, but still be secretive. It also offered the opportunity to bond with other Paranormals. Most of the circus acts were our kind. Non-human.'

Ash's stories were fascinating. I never imagined our people had been able to hide so well. Then again; I had. I guess you only see what you want to. And mortals don't want to see what they can't understand. Not unless it's in a structured and "safe" way. Like a circus.

Chapter Six

'Don't be so stupid,' Mariah said with an exasperated sigh.

'I'm not stupid.' Her comment cut Metisse deep.

I saw it happen. Old insecurities resurfaced, enhanced by the strange love triangle he was in. Never in his whole life had Metisse felt inadequate with a woman. That was the one area where he was completely sure of his prowess. As a consummate player, he'd had his pick of women. He had never been rebuked, never had his heart broken. In love, he was the aggressor. The one who ran the show. He chose.

Metisse never even entertained the idea it could be any different. This was his life. He looked good, and he knew it. He was rich and had immense power through his wealth. Doors openen. "No" wasn't a word he encountered. He got what he wanted, when he wanted it, and how he wanted it.

And then I arrived.

And screwed it all up.

As the son of the strongest Sabre leader ever, he had big shoes to fill. From an early age people judged him. The Sabre community was a critical environment to grow up in.

Especially if your heritage put you smack in the middel of the lime light.

Everything he did was put under the microscope. His every action was compared to what Charmaine would have done. What Charmaine would have said. Metisse loved his mother to death, but her strength made his life a hell of a lot more difficult.

We were in the central meeting space in the Sabre head-quarters. It was a massive circle-shaped room in the strong-hold. There was a platform of sorts with tables and chairs arranged around, and facing it. This was where all the important Clan decisions were made. It was where news was shared, celebrations took place and loss was shared. It was also where the Sabre leaders convened to discuss important matters.

Mariah had called a meeting of the Sabre council. No reason was given other than decisions needed to be made. Decisions on what?

I noticed a distinct nervousness in Metisse earlier today when he received the call. He was summoned. That meant he was not in control. And that—control—was a thing with Metisse.

'Will you go with me?' he asked in a rare moment of vulnerability.

'Sure.' What else could I have said. He looked really worried.

I wasn't looking forward to it, though I must admit I was curious. The last few times I was with the Clan, I felt a distinct animosity radiating from some of its members. It wasn't in anything they said or did. It was a feeling. Something that hung in the air.

The atmosphere was hostile as soon as we came through the door. Hard eyes followed our every step. Stern faces greeted us with barely a nod.

Mariah made no bones about her dislike for me. Not that I minded, it was mutual. I guess I stomped into her territorium. The lady had it in for me from day one.

That Metisse brought me to this meeting was an affront to her. At least that was her perspective on it. I was here to support him. Not to interfere. Whatever this was, it was Sabre business.

Charmaine greeted us warmly. Both of us. She made a point of welcoming me to the meeting, much to Mariah's chagrin.

The meeting room was packed. I think just about all the Clan adults were here. Must be something very important. What would merit this kind of a turn out?

There was a distinct tingle in my spine, and my gut told me this would not end well. The nervous way in which Metisse looked from Mariah to Charmaine compounded my feeling of dread. He felt it too.

Looking round I saw a lot of nervous fidgeting. People avoided eye contact with either Metisse or me. Me, I understood. I was still an outsider, no matter that I was half Sabre. Despite—and because of—my heritage, I would never fit in. I knew that and accepted it.

'What's this about?' Metisse asked once we were all seated.

Mariah took centre stage and addressed the clan in her strong clear voice.

'Sabre life is centred around the Clan. The Clan is all. We live and breath for the Clan and all its members.' Okay. I doubted the part about the Clan being everything. My perception was that most of the Clan members were quite egotistical, not so group-minded when it came down to the basics, but that's just my opinion.

'In our culture you are born into a Clan or you move from one to another because of a bond.'

Something told me we were getting down to the nitty gritty. The unease in my gut intensified exponentially.

'When a Clan member finds his or her soulmate, they have two options. The mate joins their clan, or they join the mate's clan. They can not be part of both.'

The big word was out.

All faces turned to Metisse who was becoming more and more nervous with very word Mariah spoke. His nostrils flared and his brow creased. His mouth was pulled to a thin line in anticipation of what was to come.

'Metisse, you have found your soulmate.' The last words were more or less spat out.

'Or half of one,' some one called from the crowd. Metisse's eyes flashed in anger at the remark and the nervous laughter in the crowd.

Mariah waited until the snickers subsided. That in itself sent a clear message that she agreed with the sentiment. She didn't interfere with the way Metisse was being riled by the Clan. I nearly did, but was stopped by a very dark look on my lover's face.

'When you take a mate outside of the clan. You—or the mate—moves,' she repeated her point.

She looked directly at Metisse.

'You need to choose. Either your mate joins our Clan, or you leave and join her's.' She challenged him.

There was a deep and painful silence. No sniggers anymore. The impact of the choice was clear to all. It wasn't just choose a clan. It was also relinquish your leadership if you don't chose this one.

Metisse's dark features were pale, the only fierce colour resided in his bright ochre eyes. All blood had dissipated from his face. He looked at his mother and then to me. I saw raw panic in his fully opened eyes and the way his nostrils flared with every deep breath.

I wanted to help him. To say how stupid this all was. Mariah demanded that I join this Clan, but they wouldn't let me or Gabriel in because of our Wolf blood. Not that we wanted to, but that was moot. It was a catch twenty-two. What ever Metisse chose, he would loose. Big time.

The silence continued. My shoulders buckled under the oppressive tension. It made me feel small.

'You have to choose,' she aimed her repeated demand directly at Metisse. 'This Clan or her's.' She pointed to me.

Oh crap.

This was going downhill in a bucket.

I hadn't foreseen anything like this when I started this strange triangle that we have; Wolves, Sabres and me.

Metisse looked at me. His eyes were open in shock and what looked like panic. I felt for him.

Another part of me wondered what he would actually choose. By the look of his face, it was about fifty-fifty at the moment. I didn't like the odds. Mind you, I didn't like that he was being forced to denounce either of the options. But this was Clan business. I had no voice in this.

I had no idea what he would choose. I hoped me, but that would almost kill him. Though, to be honest, so would the alternative.

Then it occurred to me how Mariah could be using this as a political weapon. She knew fully well Metisse couldn't live without me if he had truly acknowledged me as his soul-mate. Physically couldn't. It was impossible. The only choice he had if he wanted to live was to leave the Clan. That meant denouncing his leadership role, leaving his destiny.

I hated this back-stabbing Mariah employed to gain control of the Clan. Sure, I know tradition is important. But this was politics, pure and simple. A coup attempt. As the second-in-command she was the next in line.

Metisse realised this as well. I saw the understanding in the hardening of his face. The edge of his upper lip lifted in disdain. The long canine visible for a moment. He was backed into a corner, and he knew it.

The silence was oppressing. It felt like it stretched for an eternity.

'I choose my soul-mate,' he finally stated after a much too long silence.

The overbearing stillness prevailed. All were very much aware of the tremendous pain that one sentence caused my lover. His normal aloof manner was gone. His shoulders sagged. His eyes were closed. Tears would not be allowed. That little bit of dignity was the last thing he clutched on to. I moved closer and took his hand.

My own feelings were divided. I was happy he chose me, but so sad about the circumstances and consequences. At the back of my mind an irritating voice also reminded me it wasn't really a choice. He couldn't not choose me. Not if he wanted to live.

'You relinquish your place in this Clan?' Mariah asked, mirroring the bewilderment of the rest of the Clan.

I thought that was what she wanted; the power.

The drop of moisture at the edge of her eyes belied my previous assumption. She really hadn't contemplated Metisse would actually chose me; that our bond was a bonafied soulmate bond.

She pushed him into a choice to show his link to me wasn't as strong as he thought. Mariah, and the rest of the

Clan, clearly never seriously entertained the idea he would actually leave.

Metisse took a deep breath and squeezed my hand. He stood up straight.

'I do,' he said with a strong voice. 'I choose my soulmate.'

Silence again. People looked at each other astounded. The only one not surprised was Charmaine. She knew how deep Metisse's feelings for me were.

Kylian, the enforcer, broke the silence. 'We are sorry,' he said with real deep feeling in his voice. He touched Metisse's shoulder in support. 'We do not want to see you go.' Nods all around. Yeah, well too late for that now. You all pushed Metisse too far, and now it was done.

'You are our leader. We lose not just a Clan member, but also our chieftain.' Kylian continued.

His words weren't meant to, but they cut me deep to the bone. This was my fault. If I hadn't been here, Metisse wouldn't be in this predicament. Dread filled my stomach and I started to feel physically sick. Metisse squeezed my hand again, aware of my guilty feelings.

Kylian let go of Metisse and moved into the centre of the platform. 'We need to decide on our new leader.' Nods again. 'Mariah is the second-in-command. She is the next in line.'

'No' The voice was clear and strong. All eyes turned to Charmaine.

'Metisse was still in his first five years as the Clan leader. He leaves of his own accord. That means the chieftainship reverts back to his predecessor. To me. Until I decide who the next in line will be.' It wasn't a suggestion. It was a declaration.

Kylian looked to Mariah, as we all did. I saw a mix of anger and uncertainty in her face.

I glanced at Metisse. The corners of his lips were curled up slightly in the beginning of a smile he was desperately trying to conceal.

'Does anyone challenge my claim to the leadership?' Charmaine asked looking slowly from one to the other. I detected a few members who were not happy with the direction this was going, but no own stood up and openly challenged her. Most seemed relieved. Glad that their real leader was once again calling the shots.

'This is not the time for new leadership,' Charmaine continued as she moved her wheelchair more to the foreground. 'We are at war. We need stability and clarity.'

'This is not our fight.' The clansman I identified as Gregor stated very resolutely. He was an older Sabre. More set in his ways.

'It is,' Charmaine countered. 'It always has been. We are all paranormal creatures involved in the war with the Council'

'Things were good before she came.' Gregor pointed to me. 'Now we have lost our chieftain and we are embroiled in a war that has nothing to do with us. Let the others take care of themselves. We take care of the Clan.'

There were more nods of agreement. I guess my popularity was at an all time low in the Clan. Not just because I "stole" Metisse. Bummer.

Charmaine stared straight at Gregory. His stance wavered. He held her eye, but it cost him.

'Have you forgotten what happend the last time the Council came calling?'

There was an embarrassed silence.

'The only reason there still is a Clan is because of the

help we received then. We were assisted by others in OUR fight with the Council. That was the turning point. Without them, you would not be alive today.'

All eyes were focussed on the ground in front of them, the reprimand clear. No one, except Kylian, Metisse and myself dared to look the leader in the eye.

'This IS our fight,' she continued in a softer voice. 'We are all in this together. The peace we had was a sham. It was only as long as the Council chose to leave us alone. We were lucky. They focussed their attention on others. But they knew we were here. They have always known. Do you seriously think they will not turn their gaze to us, the strongest Sabre Clan on the continent, once again?'

Then she surprised us all.

'We have a guarded peace with the Council. They agreed to leave us alone, for the moment. Not because of our strength, but because of those around us. Those that helped us.'

She meant Ash. I was getting progressively more curious about that day, and about my friend. I would have to ask the big man later.

'It is due to our allegiances that we are what you see today. Without them, we are a direct target.'

'No,' Gregor again. The man wouldn't learn. 'The strength is the Clan. Not that abomination or the Wolves.' Another Ash- and canine hater.

'Then why didn't we win that day?' It was a simple question. 'The Clan was bigger then. We were warriors, not pampered rich kids. More attuned to fighting. Stronger than now.' Charmaine cocked her head and dared anyone to speak. 'So why didn't we win then?'

No one spoke.

This was a massive blow to the arrogance and self assurance of the Clan. They felt superior. Not just to the Wolves, but to any- and everything.

The problem wasn't that their best chieftain ever, dared proclaim their need for help. The issue was that no one could rebuke it. There was no answer other than that they would have lost.

Today was turning out to be very interesting.

'No one can take on the Council on their own,' Charmaine said, mollifying the impact of her words. 'It is too powerful, even for a Clan as strong as ours. Then, and now.'

She moved her chair around the people, taking care to acknowledge every one of them. She stopped in front of Gregor.

'My old friend,' she took his hand. 'We have fought together many times. We have won most of the conflicts. But this is one we cannot win on our own. We need help. And they need us.'

She turned to face the whole Clan. 'The Council can, and will, be defeated. We will play a big role in this. Our advice, our help and our guidance along with our warriors will turn the tide and together we will conquer. We will rid this world of the Council's oppression and terror. Then we, and all paranormals, will finally be able to live in peace.'

She moved her chair towards me and took my hands.

'Trish is the Lamaq. She is the link needed to join all paranormals together. She is the living proof Sabres and Wolves can coexist, can even complement each other. We need to work with the others. We need their help. And they need ours.'

I looked around. There was a genuine feeling of acceptance. Charmaine had done it again. She'd taken a political time-bomb and transformed it into a rally behind our joint cause.

I was so happy the Clan was still on board. Losing them would have been a major set back. I also hoped it would make Metisse feel better now the leadership reverted back to his mother.

It held the door open for what might be possible after this war. This war would throw the whole paranormal world upside down. Who knows what would happen then? What traditions would still be applicable?

Chapter Seven

We lay in bed later that night. Metisse and me.

Our lovemaking was very emotional, deep. He held me close and his touch was so tender it brought me to tears. His dedication to my pleasure was so complete it made me feel almost selfish.

Metisse undressed me slowly, stopping to kiss every spot he unveiled. Goosebumps ran up and down my whole body. Heat radiated from where his lips lightly touched my skin. I closed my eyes and let the feelings overwhelm me.

I felt every inch of my body. Every short hair he moved, every inch of my skin he touched. I felt everything, in a way I had never done before. I let myself drift on a sea of bliss as every neuron in my body screamed out in pleasure.

Metisse's restraint astounded me. His only focus was my pleasure. It made me feel so bad and egotistical. Though he made me feel sooooo good. I was torn between one emotion and the other, but he wouldn't let me turn the attention to him. He needed to please me. Needed me to be the centre of his universe.

When he finally entered me I felt a connection I'd never experienced with him before. It touched me to the very depth of my soul and I felt the tears stream down my face. Metisse stopped moving, unsure whether he was hurting me. I clung on to him, shouting out my love for him and he resumed his slow lovemaking, sending me over the edge into wave after wave of pure bliss.

In the multi colour of my pleasure I felt Metisse climax with the same overwhelming emotions I was experiencing.

Lying in each other's arms, I remember thinking this was the deepest link and the most profound emotion I ever had with Metisse. It warmed my soul. The bond was true. No matter what I thought about how much control I had, I couldn't ignore the pull we had on each other. This was destined to be. This was real. I think I finally felt what Metisse had all these months.

The nature of my bond with both of my beaus was that I shared my love. Shared my emotions. Tonight I was Metisse's alone.

And it felt wonderful.

Mesmerizing.

There was a comfortable silence for a long time and we basked in the closeness and love we both felt. Words wouldn't have added anything. Like the song says: sometimes you say more when you say nothing at all.

Metisse gave up his life for me. His future as the leader of the Clan. His standing. Everything. It was overwhelming. The depth of his love warmed me. But...

Yes that stupid "but".

But, it put an enormous pressure on me. Here I was, loving both of them. Metisse and Gabriel. I was forcing two alphas to live in a manner completely foreign to them. And to boot, I'd chosen from two species that were natural enemies.

Way to go, Trish.

Could I have made it any more complicated? Not even if I tried.

'How are you feeling?' I finally ramped up the courage to ask Metisse.

He took a while to answer. I could feel he was awake. His breathing was regular, but not slow like when he was in dreamland. Tingles of anticipation snaked up my spine and ate away at my conviction.

'Good.' He finally ended my dread. I breathed again.

Metisse kissed the top of my head and squeezed me closer. 'I do,' he continued. 'I didn't think I would to tell you the truth, but actually I'm relieved.'

I lifted my head up and looked at him. 'Relieved?'

'Yes,' he answered with a smile that warmed my soul. 'The pressure of the past moths was unbearable.'

I smiled, my head back on his chest. I was glad he couldn't see it. That was the Metisse I knew, he could be so dramatic. And I loved him for it.

'It was so difficult to balance the clan with what we are doing here, he continued. 'I felt torn all of the time. Not in loyalty. I can be loyal to both, still am. But the perspectives are so very different.'

I was surprised. This was not what I expected from my lover.

'When I'm here, I'm focussed on the fight with the Council. But when I'm there I feel disconnected with that fight and my Sabre blood boils at the thought of fighting for others than just the clan. I know, you don't have to tell me.

It's selfish. But that's what we are. You said it once before, we feel superior to all other paranormal creatures.'

'Now that pressure is gone and I can focus completely on you and the cause.'

'And that Charmaine is reinstated?'

He chuckled. 'That's the best part of it all. The clan has their strong leader, and I have you.'

He kissed me on my lips and pulled me close.

Chapter Eight

Once word was out the Lamaq was here, people of all kinds flocked to Weisland.

Not all of them made it here.

The prolonged howl jumped from one voice to another as the heart-breaking news reached even the furthest wolf in the pack. I held my breath as I recognised one voice after the other. Moses, Jacob, even the females joined in the lament. Then, there, the one tone I was searching out; Gabriel.

I closed my eyes and felt the torment in the deep tones. Goosebumps ran up and down my arms and my eyes teared up as the howl ended in an oppressive and dark silence.

I dropped everything I was doing and made my way to the bar where I first met Gabriel and the pack. The parking lot was filled with bikes and pick-ups, more arrived from all directions.

Every Werewolf in the vicinity answered the call.

The pull of the howl was intrinsic to our kind. The alpha called and we came.

I let the bike slant on the kickstand and made my way to the bar.

Gabriel appeared in the doorway just as I was about to mount the few steps. His sad eyes were a mirror to the pain and anguish I heard in his call.

My heart went out to my soulmate and I hurried up the steps to take him in my arms. He hugged me with an urgency that surprised me, even after the depth of feeling I had seen and heard. He wouldn't let me go. I felt a tremor go through his body as he burried his face in my hair. I held on tighter. Willing my strength to pass over to him.

I despaired at the thought of what news would bring on such a monumental emotional reaction from the alpha of the pack. My heart sank. It would be terrible.

With a barely audible snick I'm sure only I heard, Gabriel released me from his bear hug and stood up straight again. He took my hand in his and turned to the congregated Wolves. There were men and women here from all the packs that joined us, not just the Weisland one.

Gabriel took a deep breath and looked out over the crowd. 'We have lost a pack,' he announced.

The air was filled with shocked intakes of breath.

'The Denver pack is no more.' Gabriel paused to let the news take hold in the stunned audience.

'None?' A voice came from the left. Gabriel shook his head.

The implications of his statement were massive. No one was left of the Denver pack. No one. Not the elders, the men, women, not even the children.

A cry shattered the silence. I turned towards a couple that stood to my right at the edge of the onlookers. A man I recognised from Gabriel's pack held on tightly to a young woman. She was unable to stand on her own legs as complete anguish rolled over her frame. Her wails cut me, and everyone else, to the bone. Elisabeth originated from the Denver pack. She followed her love to Weisland many years ago, as was tradition in the Wolf packs.

Gabriel let go of my hand and walked towards the couple. The Wolves made way for him as he moved forward. Elisabeth and her mate Jacob were now kneeling on the ground. He had his arms around her in an attempt to console her. Gabriel placed his hand on Jacob and Elisabeth's shoulders and squeezed in support. Her cry continued, joined by snicks from Jacob.

Gabriel threw back his head and howled at the moon. Elisabeth and Jacob joined him. On the second howl the sky was assailed by the collective cry of more than sixty wolves. My voice joined theirs. Their pain was ours.

That our howl might scare the human inhabitants of the town was irrelevant. We physically had to voice our anguish and solidarity with our fallen kin. We had to get it out of our system before we could do anything else.

The cry finally tapered off and silence returned.

Elisabeth leaned into Jacob, her voice now still. There would be more tears, more cries. But now the initial pain was alleviated by the feeling of oneness of the packs.

Gabriel returned to the steps and mounted them again. He took my hand again and addressed the Wolves. 'The pack was attacked at twilight. The Council's assassins surrounded the homes on the reservation and went from house to house. They killed all they could find.'

'All?' Moses asked softly.

'All,' Gabriel confirmed despondently. 'They killed the pack members and any Arapaho they encountered. Thirty-two in total.'

The sheer volume of the massacre hit me like a brick

wall. Thirty-two people, human and Werewolf alike, were murdered by the Council's assassins.

We were all silent. What could we say. I descended into a barrage of guilt and anger emotions.

'A message was left,' Gabriel broke through my reverie. 'For us.' He swallowed loudly. My heart dropped. Dread pulled the muscles of my neck and back into a hard block and sent stabs of pain into my brain.

Gabriel nodded to Moses who read from a tablet he held. 'Anyone who contemplates joining the rebellion will feel the wrath of the the Council.'

'But the Denver pack wasn't part of us,' I stated confused.

'No,' Gabriel answered. 'They weren't. They hadn't even approached us. They were innocents.'

Innocents.

Not rebels. Just a pack living in peace secluded on a reservation with their Arapaho kin.

'No one is safe,' Gabriel announced, his voice strong and rousing. 'The Council murdered innocent men, women and children to stop others from joining our just cause. They rule by terror and this is yet another example of their ruthlessness and malevolence. They will stop at nothing to quell our voice and subjugate our people. This will continue. Not just now, because of us, because of our cause or even because of the prophecy. These atrocities cement their power. They will not willingly relinquish their steel grip on the paranormal world. They will pursue their tyranny until we stop them. By any means.'

He looked at each person in the crowd. Gabe's eyebrows were crunched and set his now glaring red eyes deep in shadow. His thin lips narrowed as he continued.

'The Denver pack was a peaceful pack. They were not a

party in the war between us and the Council. But the Council annihilated them anyway. No matter that they were neutral. They were massacred to make a point.' I saw more red eyes and hints of fur pushing though skin as Gabriel's words cut deep in everyone's soul.

'A clear message no one is safe from the Council. Not if they join us and not if they don't. This was meant to discourage us. To extinguish the fire of freedom before it takes hold in the paranormal world.'

There were many nods.

'It won't work. We see this for what it is. Terror. Murder. Tyranny.'

Bunched fists were punched in the air. The intense atmosphere of pain changed to one of indignation and insurrection. My blood rushed through my veins in reaction to the energy I felt. This atrocity would not work. It would not defeat our righteous goal. We would liberate our kind from the despot Cantix.

Gabriel turned to Elizabeth. 'We will avenge your family and friends. That, I promise.'

New howls split the night air. Howls of defiance. Howls that held the promise of war, and bloodlust.

These new howls would keep the good people of Weisland shivering in their beds tonight.

The Council's last act of terror back-fired on them.

We were inundated with packs who risked the journey to our compound and swelled the rebellion numbers. Gabriel sent out vanguards to protect those small family units that lived outside of regular packs and bring them back to the safety of our compound in the seemingly black hole in Aquanaris' sight.

The influx wasn't restricted to Werewolves, other paranormal creatures rightfully deduced their own safety was as fragile as that of the Wolves. Our compound of tents, trailers and mobile homes grew exponentially as it took over most of the forest to the south of Weisland.

The inhabitants of our fair town did what they always did when faced with the paranormal; they pretended not to see. Ignorance had always been a positive characteristic for the humans in this area. They chose to continue their short-sightedness and welcomed the "visitors" as a new opportunity to enhance the commerce in the town.

The forests supplied more than enough game to supplement what we bought from the townspeople. Our community thrived and a feeling of oneness prevailed.

There's nothing like a common enemy to band different species together.

Chapter Nine

There were just a few left.

Five adults and two children. All that was left of the Santa Fe Wolf pack.

They limped into the meeting location we'd agreed on in one of our few communications. Most of the adult females were wounded in one way or the other, and one of the children was carried in a sling on the sole male's back.

This was not what we expected. I looked past them, expecting more people to come out of the shrubs. Gabriel shook his head. This was it. No one else.

Dread filled me. This was it? All that was left of the eighteen people who made up the pack? What had happened? Oh shit. The Council. Again.

The man came up to me. He stared me in the eye and took a deep breath.

'You are the Lamaq?'

I nodded.

He closed his eyes, his features lost their edge and he relaxed his brow. They had made it. The relief was visible.

He couldn't speak. An older woman came up next to him and put her hand on his arm in support. He swallowed audibly and opened his eyes again. A faint smile to the woman.

'Thank you for taking us in,' she said to me. 'We have travelled long and hard.'

I nodded. I didn't know what to say?

'We are glad that you are here, Madeleine.' Ash to the rescue. The big man came over and took the woman's hand.

'Your presence here warms my heart,' she answered him with tears in her eyes. Madeline bowed her head in some kind of reverence to the Shaman. The man also nodded his head in respect to Ash. The big man's reach obviously extended deep into the south of the US.

'What happened?' he finally asked what we all didn't dare to.

The woman looked up, glanced at her companion who nodded his consent, then started her agonising tale.

'We were on our way here, the whole pack. In the past weeks there were signs we were being stalked. Strange phenomena took place on the reservation. People became ill without any cause. Our crops burned with a weird blue light. A horse gave birth to a foal without a head.'

I turned to Ash. This was beyond strange. 'Magic.' The one word said it all. Madeleine nodded solemnly.

'The elders met and we decided to leave. It was the only thing we could have done.' Nods all around again.

The man picked up the story. 'We left at night. We assumed they were looking for us. Others on the reservation filled in for us and made it look as though the pack was still there. It was dangerous for them, and we don't know if anything has befallen them. We travelled only at night. Hid by day. It went well, until yesterday. Then they caught up with us.' Madeleine squeezed his arm again.

'They attacked us just before dawn this morning, while we were getting ready to sleep. We were all very tired. Their assassins took out our guards. They were in Wolf form, but still didn't see the Council coming.'

'They must have shrouded their presence,' Madeleine added.

'You are all that is left of your pack?' Gabriel asked softly.

The man nodded. Madeleine sniffed. The pain obvious in the tears that ran down her face and pulled brown streaks where it met the sand and blood on her features.

From the corner of my eye I saw Jacob approach Gabriel. He whispered in the Alpha's ear and Gabriel's face became hard, the creases in his brow more pronounced.

He turned to me. 'Trish, we have to leave. The scouts reported fluctuations in the forest aura about half an hour from here.' I nodded. The blood running cold in my veins. He didn't have to say it out loud. It was the Council.

Everyone came into action. Ebony, one of Gabriel's pack, carefully took the child from the visitor's back. The little girl was limp and clearly in need of medical aid. 'I'll take care of her,' she said softly. 'Come, we need to leave.'

The rest of the small group were helped into the four-wheel drives we came in on. I turned to leave when I saw that the big man was lagging behind. 'Ash? Are you coming?'

'I'll follow,' he answered with a reassuring smile. 'I want to make sure they can't follow us.'

'How are you going to do that?'

He just chuckled a bit and winked. That was Ash to a tee. Mysterious. Though I had no doubt he would be able to erase our tracks. More than likely with magic. The man was an enigma. Again, I was very happy he was on our side.

I walked to the car, opened the passenger door and sat down next to Gabriel. He immediately drove us out of the clearing and deep into the forest track. This part of the forest was dense, the tracks barely accessible, even for the vehicles we brought. Taking care not to get stuck—but aware of the need for haste—Gabriel led the four car convoy out through the woods towards the hard top a mile away. We stopped just before we left the dirt track to let the three wolf scouts jump into the back of the pick up. Ash would follow on his own time. I wasn't really worried about him, but hoped he wouldn't linger too much. You never knew with the Council.

Once on the interstate we made good progress and were back at our Weisland HQ a few hours later. I was surprised, but happy to see the Shaman already waiting for us. I don't know how he always does that, but with him; expect the unexpected. It wouldn't help to ask. He wouldn't answer, at least not with something I would understand.

The Santa Fe pack was taken to our infirmary where they would be checked over by the doctor. The little girl looked slightly better, the heat in the car had taken the edge off her pale features and she now slept peacefully, her breaths deep and regular.

We would reconvene with the remnants of the pack after they had eaten and rested.

'What did you find?' I asked Ash later that night when he, Metisse, Gabriel, Jacob and myself were seated around my kitchen table, all nursing a stiff drink.

'The Council was about ten minutes behind us. You left

at precisely the right moment. Five minutes later and I might not have been able to eradicate any sign of us or the Santa Fe pack. It was close as it was.'

'Did you see them?' Jacob asked.

Ash nodded. 'There were ten of them. Most assassins, with a wizard.'

Assassins. A year ago, that might have been me. I felt a distinct guilt for the massacre that happened. No, I hadn't done it. But it was too familiar.

'That explains the magic,' Gabriel brought me out of my reverie.

'They won't follow us,' Ash stated very clearly. I cocked my head. Was that because there were no tracks anymore, or no assassins? He just smiled that aggravating, evasive way he always does. One day, I would say something about it. Yeah, and he would laugh. So, not much use really. I left it open. If he wanted to tell us, he would. Need to know. With Ash, it was always "need to know".

A thought occurred to me. 'It's too much of a coincidence the Council came down on the pack just days after they approached us to join the cause.'

More nods. I don't believe in coincidence. Just so you know.

'Do you think they might have hacked the communication one way or the other?' I aimed my question at Jacob. He was the resident IT geek. He shook his head.

'Not possible,' he stated. 'But I'll check, just to be sure.'

Another thought crossed my mind. 'Who else knew about it?' I didn't like where this was gong. I'm not a trusting person to start off with. Okay, I'm paranoid. And this potentially looked like betrayal.

'Not many people, I think,' Gabriel answered, about as happy as I was about the implications.

'You're thinking of a traitor?' Ash asked.

'I suppose I am,' I answered, feeling dejected.

'We have work to do then,' Gabriel commented. 'To find out who it is.'

'Yes,' Ash chimed in. 'But carefully. We don't want to spook whoever it might be.'

Metisse was the silent one in the conversation. He stood to the side with that slightly arrogant smile on his face that said it all: "It's not one of mine." Yeah, well don't be too sure of that. It could be anyone. Sometimes I wanted to wipe that pretentious smirk off his face.

'Get your enforcers in here first thing tomorrow,' I said, maybe a bit too directly. 'We need to get to the bottom of this quickly. Maybe it is a coincidence, but we need to be sure.'

Nods all around. They all finished their drinks and, except Gabriel, everyone left my house.

We'd see what tomorrow would bring.

Chapter Ten

The enforcers were gathered in the Wolves' Biker Bar at nine sharp next morning. Early, especially after last night. Gabriel and I didn't get to bed before two. And sleep only came an hour later.

There were four of them.

Three wolves and Kylian from the Sabre Clan. This was actually something the two species had in common. Packs and clans alike, all had an enforcer. I guess it's inherent to our way of life. Hiding in plain site necessitates discipline and someone has to enforce it.

It isn't a popular job. Not by any standards. These three men and one woman were seasoned warriors. All of them had been around for a long time and seen it all probably. All had done what was necessary, no matter how difficult or bloody that was. These were not people you could push over. Or easily pull the wool over their eyes. This group was seriously experienced and bad-ass. They had to be.

'You saying we have a traitor in our midst?' Elroy, the New Orleans pack enforcer started the meeting.

'No,' Gabriel answered and looked at each of them individually. 'We're saying; we might have one.' He dared anyone to contradict him. These tough people didn't take any shit, well neither did we. Gabriel brought it as the strong Alpha he was.

There were nods all around. They acknowledged his dominance. Even Kylian, but I think that's more because the two of them got along quite well. I was glad the Clan was represented here. If they had been absent it would have sent the wrong message; that they thought they were superior to betrayal. Superior being the most important part of that sentence.

'Your investigations have to be low key. We don't want to start a witch hunt,' Gabriel continued. I left it to him. With the Wolves in the majority here, he was the best person to lead this meeting. 'It's possible this is a coincidence.'

The packs and the clan were on a guarded coexistence at the moment. The common goal was what set centuries of mutual animosity to the side. The Council was the true enemy. A traitor could upset the fragile balance.

We agreed the enforcers would each conduct their own investigation and get back to Gabriel and Ash with the results by tomorrow end of day. The main point of attention was the Santa Fe pack. Who knew about them and their decision to join the cause? That would be the starting point.

Kylian stayed back with Ash and me after the meeting. I liked him. He was one of the few clan members who welcomed me when I first met the Sabres. He was also the one who advocated working with the Wolves and I was thankful to him for that.

'You okay?' he asked me.

I smiled. 'Yes, thanks. It just cuts me up thinking

someone could betray us. I guess that's naive, but I just never even entertained the idea.'

'No, me neither,' he answered. 'I hate to think what will happen if it turns out to be true.'

'Let's not get ahead of ourselves,' Ash brought us back down to earth. 'It might be nothing. A coincidence. Nothing more.'

'Yeah.'

It was obvious in Ash's raised brow he didn't believe my agreement.

'I'll check within the clan,' Kylian continued. 'I don't think anyone there knew about the pack. No one other than Metisse and he is definitely not a traitor.'

That comment shocked me. No, of course Metisse wasn't a traitor. He couldn't be. No more than Gabriel, Ash or me. How could that even be a consideration?

Kylian noticed my shock and was quick to add, 'Metisse is not a suspect. Believe me, he is not even under consideration. His loyalty was never a question. I should have made that clear up front. I meant I do not expect a traitor in the clan as no one knew about the Santa Fe pack. Sorry, Trish.' He placed his hand on my arm in support. 'I didn't mean to upset you.'

I shook my head, a bit embarrassed at my reaction. I shouldn't be so overly sensitive. 'Thanks, Kylian. It's okay.' He smiled and winked.

Kylian nodded to Ash and me, picked up his phone, and left the meeting room.

Only Ash and me remained.

'You okay?' his turn to ask the same question.

I thought about it for a moment. A year ago I would have answered it differently, but then again, my life now wasn't anything like what it had been then.

'Yeah,' I answered. 'I'm okay. Still getting used to all of this.' He smiled and nodded. 'Life used to be simple.' I laughed.

'Not really. Just looked that way.'

'Uh huh.' We sat in a comfortable silence for a while.

Something had been bothering me for a while and was actually enhanced by the possibility of a traitor in our ranks. Ash noticed my internal turmoil and raised one brow in question.

'Ash,' I started, searching for the right words. 'The Council knows where we are.'

He nodded.

'They know that we have our stronghold here in Weisland.'

Again a nod.

'If there is a traitor, then they probably know how many of us there are. It seems they know which packs and clans have joined us anyway.' More nods.

'So why don't they attack us?' There, that was what was bothering me. The Council attacked the packs and clans that wanted to join us, but they left us alone. Why?

'Multiple reasons, I think,' the big man answered. 'We can be sure they know where we are and also have a quite good idea of our size and strength.'

My turn to nod now.

Ash brought his hands together, the long fingers and thumbs meeting at the top and forming a tent-like pattern.

'The Council is waiting it out for now. They want to see who rebels against them. An attack on us will force any other dissents underground. They want to stamp out all rebellion.'

Okay, sounds logical.

'They also can't afford a war.'

Now I was surprised, Ash noticed and explained further.

'Cantix has never gone to war. His tactic is to quash any resistance before to comes to a large conflict. This is new for him. Cantix came to power through trickery and deceit. He is a political creature. A tyrant, not a general. Strategy is not his strongest skill. He attacks the boundaries, the packs and clans on the periphery of our cause. He shows the others that they are not safe. That he can—and will—get to them before they find sanctuary with us. His reign is one of terror. For that he cannot confront us head on. That would require military strategy, which he does not have.'

'But there are soldiers, generals, in his army.'

'There are, but they would have a big challenge convincing him to go to war.' Ash countered. 'Plus, an all-out conflict would expose us to humans. The secret Cantix is so desperate to hide would be out in the open. Small bands of Native Americans can disappear without making the news. They are in a world of their own and not news-worthy to the general public in the US, or worldwide for that matter. Their demise would only touch others of their own kind. Us. The Native Americans and the paranormals. And serve as a deterrent for any potential rebellious notions of other packs.'

He placed his hands on the arm rests of the chair.

'Most of the sabres, with the exception of Metisse's clan, live on the boundaries of human society too. Their interaction is generally restricted to the family unit. Cantix needs to keep our worlds separate. This is the basis of his power over our kind. The historic distrust humans have for anything out of the ordinary has left deep rifts in our society. We all believe we need to be invisible to survive.'

This was a lot deeper than I imagined.

'And.' Ash pulled me out of my reverie. 'There is you.'

'Me?'

'Yes. This is the first time the paranormal fractions feel any kind of unity. They rally behind one person: you. You have done what no one else has been able to achieve. You brought former adversaries together in a common cause. You convinced sworn enemies to lay aside their animosity and join forces against the real foe. You are the product of a before unforeseen coalition. Your impact on the struggle is monumental. Not just because you are the Lamaq. Or because you are half Wolf and half Sabre, but also because you have recognised mates from both species as your soulmate. It is a confirmation of the connection. This love triangle you have is part of the whole prophecy. It strengthens the pull and is therefore even more dangerous to the Council.'

Wow. That was a lot to process. Not only was I the Lamaq, it seems the guys were also part and parcel of the whole prophecy. I was going to have fun explaining that to them. It might even stop their constant bickering. A smile crept onto my face.

This was turning out to be an interesting conversation.

'They don't dare attack us?' Just checking.

'Not yet, no.'

Not yet, hmm. Back down to earth.

'They will not attack us outright if they can help it. So their tactics will be stealth and to hack away at the support we might get. They will continue to make examples of those who contemplate joining forces with us. That way they hope to minimise our size and power. Stealth will also allow them to eat away at our numbers from the inside out. Joining our cause does not only have consequences for the pack themselves, it also radiates out to their family and friends. Terror will eat away at allegiances. Their actions strengthen the grip they have on the paranormal world. They make examples of their enemies. Of our companions. Their brutality shows that the power of the Council's magic reigns supreme.'

'Terror. The Council's power is made up of terror and blood,' I said. Ash nodded his agreement. 'Yet still people flock to us. They lay their lives in our hands,' I added.

'They do. And we have a monumental responsibility.'

I smiled at him, so happy that he emphasised the "we" in that last sentence. It was OUR cause. Not just mine. It didn't rest solely on my shoulders, even if it did feel that way sometimes.

There was one more thing that bothered me.

'If they did attack. Wouldn't they have the overhand because of their magic? And the dragons?'

There, that was what was really at the root of my nervousness. Dragons. These mystical creatures were—are —real. They are twice as frightening as you may imagine and ten times more destructive. They could sway any battle, so why hadn't the Council used them? They could make small work of our band of revolutionaries.

'There is only one dragon left,' he answered to my surprise and enormous relief.

'Only one?'

'One that we are certain about. The red dragon. It is the last confirmed dragon in existence. The council controls it, though with difficulty.'

'Confirmed?' A nagging feeling started again at the base of my spine. I didn't appreciate the kind of ambiguity I was hearing. Was there one? Or were there more?'

'There are rumours about a second dragon. A gold one. Though no sighting has ever been confirmed. It could just be another Council strategy to install fear in people.'

'But we don't know for sure that it is a rumour?'

'No, not for sure. Not one hundred percent.'

'Any more than these two?'

'No. No more.'

'No surprises? Hidden eggs anywhere?' I asked. Just to be sure.

Ash laughed. 'No eggs. You have been reading too many books or watching too many films. Dragons do not hatch from eggs. They are older than time. And like us elementals, they cannot reproduce.'

Phew. That was a relief.

One dragon was enough to give me permanent goose bumps. More would constitute nonstop nightmares.

'Thanks Ash.' I would sleep well tonight.

'We need to take this potential betrayal seriously, Trish.' He brought me back down to earth. 'They will try to break us from the inside out. We need to make sure now—and in the future—they cannot get a hold on us that way.'

'Let's wait for what the enforcers come up with. Then we'll take it from there. Okay?'

'Yes. And I will keep my eyes open.'

'Thanks.'

There was lot to think about.

The report next day offered no potential candidates. The enforcers were all adamant they had vetted their groups without any sign of a traitor. We ruled it a coincidence. It felt unresolved to me, but there was nothing I could do about it.

We would remain vigilant.

Just because there wasn't a traitor now, didn't mean there wouldn't be one in the future.

Chapter Eleven

Not all the packs joined without a struggle.

This alpha was big. Tall and wide. Most of it flab, though that could be wishful thinking on my part. If push came to shove, he would be a formidable opponent.

His rough face was bordered by an unkept beard and wild, jet-black hair with an occasional grey streak. His clothes echoed those of Gabriel's pack: jeans, t-shirt and a leather jacket. Only his were dirty and a lot worse for wear. The pack sported the same attire.

Stephan—the Alpha of the Chicago pack— greeted Gabriel in a guarded manner. Friendly, but with reluctant reverence, the slight bow only apparent if you looked for it. Then he turned and observed the other Wolves, daring them to step out of line.

As I expected; he barely glanced my way; he probably dismissed me as a lowly female.

His gaze landed on Ash and I saw his eyes squint and his lips pull into a thin hard line. Okay, there was bad blood there. Ash remained his own chill self from his position leaning against a tree, and smiled at the newcomer. There was just a hint of contempt in the smile. Not by accident. Ash never did anything by accident. I wondered what the history was on this. I'd find out sooner or later. For now I had to convince this brute to join us, him and his motley pack.

The Alpha turned to Gabriel, his back to me. 'Okay, what's all this about then? The rumour is that you're taking on the Council.' His smile was almost as wide as his face. 'About time someone did something about it.' Gabriel just nodded.

'So what's the plan?'

'Don't ask me.' Gabriel smiled.

The guy was taken back. His brow scrunched and his thick black eyebrows met in the middle of his face to form one long bushy overhang over his brown eyes.

He briefly looked at his Beta, a much smaller and older man. Still fit and muscular for his age, the beta was almost invisible next to this giant. He shrugged. His boss looked around again, once more his gaze fell on Ash, but the big man just stared back, the smile stuck to his lips. No, not Ash.

'Aren't you the Alpha of this megapack?' Gabriel shook his head and nodded to me.

The man turned his head to look who Gabriel meant. His gaze quickly travelled over me to the men standing near. A snarl escaped his lips when he became aware of Metisse. My feline lover returned the stare and Stephan's gaze passed on. Confused, he retraced his steps and looked at me again. He cocked his head as I stared back, a small crooked smile turned the edges of my mouth upwards. Understanding flowed into his thick skull and his eyes opened wide in surprise.

'A bitch?'

Gabriel hissed back; 'watch it, Stephan. She's the Chosen One. You will show respect.'

'Chosen One, my ass.' The big man laughed out loud, the sound cold and chilling.

I stood my ground. Not reacting at all, a condescending smile plastered to my face. I was acutely aware that how I handled this would determine not only whether the Chicago pack joined our cause, but also the standing of Gabriel and his Wolves. There was a lot riding on this meeting.

Stephan turned back to Gabriel, the laugher still echoing in the forest clearing. 'Get real,' he challenged Gabriel. 'A Chosen One? Do you have any idea how stupid you sound?' The tension in the air increased exponentially.

To his credit, Gabriel remained calm and just stared at his adversary. His eyes belied his calm exterior; the red slowly took over from the soft grey I knew so well.

'Are you nuts?' Stephan tried again. He sniffed the air, turned, took a step towards me and sniffed again. 'Or are you fucking her? That the reason for your insanity?'

The Wolves from Gabriel's pack slowly gathered behind their leader; their eyes bright red as fur began to push through the skin of their faces and hands.

Snarls were met by the same from Stephan's companions, with the exception of the Beta. He turned towards me, caught my eyes and looked deep into them. There was recognition there. Maybe not for me, but for someone else. My father. He nodded ever so slightly.

Peter; the Beta, took a step towards Stephan and put his hand on the big man's arm, an action that earned him a vicious look.

'Her father is Ishmael,' he stated calmly, not in the least impressed by the threatening gaze of his alpha.

Stephan turned to face me. He stared into my eyes. I returned the stare. His were blood red. The excitement of a pending fight pushed the blood forward and fuelled a shift that was imminent.

'Ishmael?' he repeated. I stayed silent. Let him make the connections.

He turned back to Gabriel. 'She's Ishmael's cub?'

Gabriel nodded. No words were needed.

The Alpha turned back to me. With three steps of his long powerful legs he was up in my face. Barely a metre from me, he towered over my form. His gaze as he looked down on me was half amusement and half aggression.

'So the old wolf had a daughter. Who would have thought?' He reached out and touched my hair, picked up a lock and let it slowly fall through his fingers. His top lip curled upwards in an attempt to locate pheromones. He sniffed. Nothing. Slowly he walked around me, his body uncomfortably close to mine.

'The daughter of a First One. And not bad to boot. How did that ugly old Wolf ever father something as pretty as you.' Lust pushed the red of his eyes to the background and I swear drool started to congeal at the edge of his mouth.

It didn't improve his features.

I stood my ground. Backing down, or one wrong comment, would light the powder keg between the packs and cause mayhem. All the Wolves were on high alert. The proximity of the Sabres wasn't helping either. Stephan had to act obnoxious, it was expected of him in the Wolf culture. Women were not in positions where they could lead, or tell men what to do for that matter.

He turned back to Gabriel, a smirk on his lips. 'Not that I don't understand,' he began, taking another step and mimicking my hour glass figure with his hands. Gabriel just stood there, his arms crossed over his chest. His demeanour outwardly calm.

'She's hot. And the daughter of one of the First. That must be one hell of a kick, fucking this one.' Stephan paused for effect. There was none from Gabriel. The packs collectively sucked in their breath at the blatant bad manners Stephan showed. He was goading Gabriel. Thankfully with no result…yet.

He upped the game. 'Still doesn't explain why she's in charge. You're supposed to be the big famous Gabriel. Ultimate leader of the Waisland pack. Not a pussy-whipped cub pining for a bitch in heat.' The last words were spat out.

I saw and felt the effect his words had on Gabriel. His eyes coloured bright red, small tufts of fur pushed through on his hands and in the base of his neck, he kept the change from his face, but only barely.

You could have heard a pin drop. No one dared to breath. This was an ultimate insult. He'd challenged Gabriel's masculinity. There was no way I could intervene without worsening the situation. If I stood up for Gabriel, it would only confirm Stephan's provocations. I ached to jump in, but one glance at Gabriel convinced me to hold my tongue.

His voice was almost a whisper, but it carried like a shout in the absolute silence of the clearing.

'Watch your tongue, Stephan,' Gabriel said calmly, the tone of his words cut through with absolute menace and the promise of unbearable pain. He stared straight into his adversary eyes and dared him to take the next step and attack. They were almost the same hight, Gabriel maybe an inch taller, and though Stephan was heavier, my bet was on the much fitter and more composed Gabriel.

Minutes felt like hours while the two stared each other down. No one moved. Not even Metisee. Even he grasped the severity of the situation. I could feel him ten paces behind me, anxious to come protectively closer if things turned haywire.

Finally, Stephan backed down. He lowered his eyes and broke the extreme concentrated battle of wills that was going on between them.

He turned back to me and looked me up and down while he slowly licked his lips. He had lost face with all present and needed to regain some of it, if he were to continue as alpha of his pack. In the Werewolf world, you were only Alpha if you were the strongest. The best. The rebuff he experienced here by acknowledging Gabriel was still superior would have to be amended.

His eyes shone wickedly and a sinister smile pulled the edges of his lips up. He glanced at Gabriel, then back to me. Stephan swaggered towards me, his bravura once again apparent. The man had a plan. Not good, whatever it was.

'So you're the Alpha?' He aimed his questions at me. I just blinked. There was no need to actually answer him. He continued his advance and stopped much too close to me for either comfort or respect. He was trying to impress me. Bully me probably. Good thing I don't impress easily. Specially not by the likes of this big lug.

'You lead this motley crew, huh?' His gaze encompassed all those present in the clearing, with the exception of his own pack, who started to warm up to their leader's posturing. There were some smiles, an occasional smirk from the Chicago pack. In the corner of my eye I saw Gabriel tense again. His brow creased as he tried to fathom what Stephan was up to.

'Not the Wolf way,' Stephan continued. 'No, not at all. A pack led by a bitch.' Gabriel flinched at the word but thankfully held his calm. 'Not even a real Wolf pack. Not with the kitties.' He smiled his challenge to Metisse and the Clan members.

I willed my other lover to stay calm.

'Even that!' His voice dripped venom as he pointed to Ash. The big man was still in a comfortable pose leaning against the tree, his arms crossed over his chest and a smile on his lips. Ash was not impressed, not in the least. That gave me some extra comfort and I willed myself to stay calm and impassive.

'You flaunt traditions here,' the humour was gone from Stephan's tone. 'This is not the Wolf way. It's a disgrace.' He stopped his pacing and stood directly in front of me. He towered over me, his upper torso inclined towards me in a menacing manner.

My lack of reaction angered him even more. I raised an eyebrow and stared him in the eye.

'And you. You are the daughter of one of the First. Of Ishmael, our great example. The first leader of all Wolves. The one who brought us to this land. And now you—of all people—you disgrace his memory by your blatant disrespect of the ancient ways.' There was a collective gasp from the onlookers.

I sensed Metisse ready to attack, and saw Gabriel move forward from his position, his arms no longer crossed over his chest, but hanging down by his side in the first throws of a full change.

The reprieve came from an unexpected corner.

'You're still the consummate bully, aren't you, Stephan?

Still don't know your place. Always trying to push where you should not.' Ash's strong voice came through the tension and stopped both my lovers and Stephan in their tracks.

The momental break in Stephan's demeanour showed the impact Ash had on the alpha. His resolve seemed to waver as his gaze flitted to the big man, his pack and then back to me.

'Shut the fuck up, you freak,' he tried to project all the menace he felt in his words, but I detected a slight nervous undertone. 'You have no say here. This is Wolf business.'

'Ash is part of this pack,' I intervened. That earned me a dark stare. Behind the threatening attitude I glimpsed insecurity. Ash certainly had an impact on Stephan. Again I wondered at the origin. That would come later. Now this tense situation had to be diffused one way or the other. I was about to talk when Stephan shouted out the point of his plan.

'You are the Alpha. The leader. Though you mock tradition, I do not. My pack lives by the old rules. Ishmael's enemies are our enemies.' Again he stared at the Sabres.

Someone should tell him he had his facts mixed up here. I was the living proof Ishmael and at least one of the Sabres had gotten on quite famously.

'We live by claw and fang,' he continued viciously. Gabriel's eyes opened to the max. He gasped. I cocked my head, not aware of the severity of Stephan's words and why they had Gabriel so riled up.

The smirk on Stephan's face was mean and diabolical. 'I call on the right to challenge.'

Okay, so that was it. A challenge.

He glared at Gabriel, then back to me. 'I challenge the

Alpha of this pack to a duel for the leadership of both packs.' He pointed to me to emphasis his demand.

He was challenging me.

Gabriel stood beside me. His whole stance one of protectiveness and anger. He would die for me, I know that. But I couldn't let that happen. I know enough of the Were-wolf traditions to understand I could not let someone else fight for me. I could not call on a champion. It was Alpha against Alpha. I knew, Gabriel knew and Stephan knew. Everyone here in the clearing did. I would have to fight a man more than twice my weight and at least fifteen centimetres taller than me. He had a lot of bulk that could give him the upper hand, but I'm quick and have the feline advantage. One he seemed blissfully unaware of.

'I accept your challenge.' My voice was clear and calm and carried over the clearing, instantly silencing the buzz Stephan's challenge had caused.

'Trish,' I heard behind me. I ignored Metisse. I loved him for his concern, but this had to be done.

Gabriel cocked his head at me in question whether I really wanted to do this. He was just as anxious as Metisse.

The only one who remained the epitaph of calm was Ash. The smile on his lips had grown and he was genuinely enjoying the prospect of me fighting the massive alpha. That strengthened me. There was no way Ash would be comfortable with this challenge if he wasn't convinced I could win. He believed in me, which meant I did too.

'Again, Stephan. Your arrogance bites off more than you can chew.' Ash stated calmly, only aggravating the man even more. I joined Ash in the smile, my apparent calm unnerving the big bully.

Gabriel lightly touched my arm in support. I appreciated the gesture and smiled at him. It was okay. I'd fight this bully. And win.

My acceptance and Ash's comment caused cracks in the veneer of Stephan's confidence.

He looked mad as hell, his eyes bright red. The tufts of fur showed on his cheeks and his brow was now one solid dense mass of fur. His lips were slightly parted and I saw the large incisors as they dropped down from his gums. He strained against the change with balled fists. His feet were planted strongly on the ground and his torso was slightly hunched, ready for the transformation.

I calmly took off my coat and gave it to Gabriel with a smile. I flexed my arms and walked into the centre of the clearing, where I waited for his first move.

Again, my self confidence caused him to waver. But there was no going back for him now. He'd dug this hole and now he would suffer the consequences.

I continued to stare at him, daring him to attack me.

It didn't take long. His brawn won the battle with the tiny bit of sense he possessed, and he charged me; throwing his whole bulk into the attack.

I side-stepped easily and he hurtled past me, much to the amusement of Gabriel's pack. I turned to face him again and waited for his next move. Again he attacked, though this time without the forward momentum that carried him past me. He expected me to duck again and was completely surprised when I took a step forward instead and ducked under his flailing fist and landed my own deep into his sternum just above his flabby belly. He went down like a ton of bricks, gasping for air.

I could have gone in for the kill while he was incapacitated, but that would not defuse the whole situation. It would be perceived as a lucky strike. No more than that. I had to beat him fair and square. Fully, more than once. I had to show it was my skill, not good luck that bested him.

So, I waited until he regained his breath. He glared at me. The insult of me waiting for him to recover was clear to both him and everyone around us. My calm demeanour compounded the affront.

Stephan growled. A deep sound that originated from his barrel chest and rose up through his fanged mouth and open sparred nostrils.

He was piping mad. Just how I wanted him to be.

Any semblance of common sense went out the window as he changed into his Wolf in one fluid motion.

I did the same, my clothes falling to the ground around me. We circled each other in Wolf form, both looking for a way into the defenses of the other.

The change made it all the more serious. Now weapons —fangs and claws—joined the fight. It was no longer only about wits and strength. I closed myself off from the calls and howls around me and concentrated fully on the massive black wolf in front of me. The long yellowish-white fangs seemed larger than most I'd encountered and the drool dripping off them emphasised my opponent's fury. Anger that would cause him to make mistakes.

He attacked.

His fangs only just missed my flank as he twisted in mid-air and changed tactics. Now I was surprised. As the Wolf he made better decisions. I should have factored the canine instinct into the equation. I berated myself for underestimating him.

He attacked again, I watched his eyes carefully and managed to evade his jaws, though his claws raked fur off my back leg. Not what I wanted.

He was ecstatic, sniffed at the fur and drooled. The jaws

curled up as he showed his fangs and went in for the kill. I stood my ground and we tumbled head over heels over the ground, snapping at each other.

I landed a good bite to his left shoulder and he yelped. I let go immediately and went in for another bite to the right side. He parried and we continued to roll over each other. This was a contest of strength and sooner or later I would lose. I knew this, and so did he. He tried harder to pin me to the ground or at least hold on to me so that he could use his size advantage.

It was time to stop this carnival. I bent into his paws and flipped us over so I stood over his body and he was on his side and back. He snapped at me and flailed in an attempt to get the upper hand.

Just as he was about to throw me off him I changed into my feline form.

Now I had the advantage. Not only in weight, but also in strength and definitely in number of wicked weapons. My claws were infinitely sharper and much longer, extending deep into his shoulders where I pinned him to the ground. My incisors were much, much bigger, true sabres. My back legs and my bulk prevented him from gaining any traction with his hind legs.

I grabbed him by the throat, my enormous canines closing around his neck. I stopped just short of ripping his throat out. He continued to struggle and refused to give up. I'm not sure if that was bravura, stubbornness or just simple fear.

'Yield, Stephan!' Gabriel stood next to us. The Wolf continued his useless struggle. I had him. One clean bite and he was dead. There was absolutely nothing he could do about it.

His demise was imminent.

'Stephan. There's no disgrace in yielding to the Lamaq.' This voice belonged to Peter, the older and much wiser beta I saw earlier. He knew. He understood the moment Gabriel called me the Chosen One.

Stephan froze. His eyes bulged and his jaws clamped shut audibly. He changed in one fluid motion and I found myself pinning a large flabby, hairy and very naked man beneath my paws. I slowly backed off, my jaws closed and the claws retracted. I remained a metre from him as the cat. I didn't trust him for one moment.

His voice was a whisper. 'The Lamaq.' It wasn't a question. I guess he needed to say it out loud. His eyes were still wide open.

The Beta handed Stephan his clothes, but he just stared at me. Not aware of anything else around him. His companion nudged him and broke his concentration. He meekly took the jeans and jacket and dressed. The t-shirt had ripped in the change.

Contrary to what is portrayed in human films, shapeshifters cannot change in and out of clothes. They rip or fall off when we change to our animal form. We need to dress again in something once we change back. This occasionally leads to embarrassing moments, as you can imagine. It makes us creative about the kind of clothes we wear. A lot of stretch to adjust when our body changed, or tough leather.

We also lose a lot of garments.

I remained in feline form. I was making a point. Not just to Stephan, to all his pack. This was the new order. This was how it would be from now on.

It dawned on me this whole Lamaq thing was potent. The impact that one word had on Stephan was massive. More even than me changing into the cat. Up to now it seems I'd grossly underestimated the reaction my dual heritage engendered. I slowly understood the possibilities the age old prophecies gave us. We really needed to milk it to the max to get the support we needed.

Gabriel came over to me holding my clothes. He stood to the right side and waited for me to decide what I wanted to do. Metisse joined us on my left. Both of my beaus supported me. To the right I also saw Ash. The big man left his perch against the tree and moved closer during the fight. The edges of his lips were still curled up in the smile that never left his face during the battle. The kaleidoscope of colours in his strange eyes calmed me, as they always do. I sat back on my haunches and let the reverse change come over me.

I ignored the stares as I took my clothes and dressed again. I clasped the belt with my knives over my leather pants and top and slid into my boots. Nothing had ripped during the change. Probably because it started as the Wolf. My clothes were all still usable.

Finally, I turned and looked at Stephan. His stance was slightly haunched, his shoulders dropped and his arms hung by his side. His gaze was locked onto me. The red had disappeared from his eyes, replaced by deep brown and yellowish-white.

I cocked my head and smiled. A small tick began in his left eye. He blinked uncontrollably, and wouldn't look at me anymore. He lowered his head. I could see his mouth working, trying to form words but unable to. Finally, he managed to voice what was expected of him in Werewolf tradition.

'You bested me in battle.' His voice was hardly audible. Stephan swallowed hard. 'The pack is yours.' His stance deflated even more.

'No.' I surprised him. 'I do not want to lead your pack.

They have a perfectly good leader now. I am not your enemy, Stephan.' He looked up at me, surprise and disbelief warring in his features. 'My wish is that we partner. Join forces to take on the real enemy; the Council.'

I took a step forward. His initial reaction was to step back, but he stopped himself.

'I don't want to kill you, or any other Wolf. You have your pack's loyalty. That is where it should stay. I want yours. Not to me, to the cause.'

'You are the Lamaq. The Chicago pack will follow you everywhere, with or without me.'

'I would prefer with you as its alpha.'

'Why?'

I cocked my head in question.

'Why let me live? You won. You, and my pack, have the right to kill me or banish me. It's the Wolf way.'

'You are no use to me dead or banished. Or to anyone else. Your pack needs you. Our war needs you. Stay and help me achieve freedom for all paranormal creatures.'

'It's not up to me,' he answered sadly. He turned towards his pack. 'I lost an alpha challenge. I no longer have a claim to the leadership of the Chicago Wolves.'

Peter stepped forward and placed his right hand on Stephan's shoulder. 'You fought with honour.'

Okay, we might have different opinions on that, but I let it go.

'There is no disgrace in the outcome of the challenge. She is the Lamaq. No one can best her.'

I hoped he was right, but was secretly sure that was an exaggeration. Talk about expectation management.

'You are our Alpha. Now, and in the future. I stand beside you. As do we all.' Peter turned to his fellow pack members. 'Is there anyone of you who thinks otherwise?' he challenged them. There were a few who looked at each other, uncertainty on their faces. Then as one they bowed to Stephan.

The beta turned back to his alpha, a massive smile on his face. 'We all do.'

The tension in the air dissipated immediately.

Later that evening, as we were all gathered around the camp fire—Wolf and Sabre alike—we spoke about the plans to bring down the Council.

Beer flowed easily and so did conversation. There was still a distinctly canine and feline side to the seating arrangements, but at least the hostile glares of earlier were absent.

'You forgot to tell me about the cat.' Stephan joked.

'You could have known.' Peter answered, just as amused. 'She is the Chosen One, the one from the prophecy.'

'Yeah, but I hadn't actually linked that with the Lamaq.'

'Different prophecy in mind, I guess?'

'Yeah, something like that.' We all laughed.

'She played dirty. Cheated.' Stephan was still stroking his wounded ego.

'No.' Gabriel answered resolutely. 'She just beat you, fair and square. She made use of all her assets, like you did. Only she won. With anything necessary. The Wolf way.'

Chapter Twelve

'So what's the bad blood between you and Stephan?'

'I helped someone once and he didn't agree.'

'Charmaine? When she was wounded by Cantix?'

Ash raised and eyebrow and smiled. 'Yes, how did you know?'

'Charmaine said someone special intervened and saved her life. Then she turned up at the clearing on the day our quest started. It was very obvious you two have quite the history together. I just put one and one together.'

He smiled at me. It lit up his face. His eyes did their multicolour kaleidoscope thing, and I felt warm inside.

'We do. When the clan came to Weisland it was Wolf territory. The pack was large then, like now. It was the strongest Wolf pack in the whole country. They were not used to competition. Their territory was rich with game, there were few humans and they thrived. The arrival of a competing group—and of a feline persuasion to boot—was not appreciated,' he continued.

I could imagine how that had gone down. Sabres invading the Wolf's domain.

'Did they announce their arrival or try to negotiate a cooperation?'

Ask laughed a hollow laugh. 'Not exactly, no.' his smile disappeared almost as quickly as it came.

'The Sabres were arrogant. Though they had been chased for many years they retained their superiority complex. Even Charmaine at that time. They came, they saw and decided to conquer. The Sabres were more warriors then. Most people were. It was about two-hundred years ago'

That's the thing about paranormals. We're basically immortal, so it's almost impossible to guess anyone's age.

'The Wolves reigned here, but they did that by tooth and claw. Not by their intellect. It was brawn and blood. The strongest had the power.'

'The Sabres were—and are—much more political, if you like. They instigated, back-stabbed. Anything to break the power of the pack from within. Initially they came as friends. They sought a connection, agreed to pay tribute and slowly worked their way into the communities here. Both the paranormal and the human worlds. Then they started their real agenda and set brother against brother. Daughter against mother.'

Hmmm. That explained a lot. Wolves were "what-you-see-is-what-you-get". Sabres were the opposite. I appreciated the cultured manners of the Sabres, but hated that I always had to have eyes in the back of my head. Somehow —with a few exception—I never really trusted them. They would just as easily stab me in the back than help if it was in their best interest. At least that part I recognised.

'When did the Wolves find out the clan was doing this?'

'When your father and I returned from our wanderings. We saw what was happening because we hadn't grown into the situation. We were immune to the provocation and instigation. Ishmael was livid. He confronted the Sabre leaders. Charmaine was the second-in-command then, her father the clan leader. The meeting did not go well. The Sabres' arrogance and supposed superiority led them to openly deride and taunt the Wolves. They laughed unabashedly at the way they'd played their enemies. How they had deceived them.'

'The Wolves were astounded. Not only at the audacity of the ones they called their friends but also at the obvious contempt the Sabres had for them.'

'Were you there?' I asked, already knowing the answer. He nodded.

'The emotions were heated and it got completely out of control very quickly. I tried to intervene, but neither side listened to reason anymore. The ensuing battle resulted in many casualties on both sides. Many were killed in that fight and the frequent skirmishes after that. Charmain's father was one of them. One of the splinter Wolf packs was responsible for his death as a reaction to the clan attacking the dens when the warriors were out. The clan used deceit to lure them out and then attacked the remaining pack members. Most of Stephan's family died in the massacre that resulted. It cemented the bad blood between the packs and the clan.'

'How did the fighting stop?'

'Charmain came to power after her father was killed. She initially continued the fighting but I was able to convince her all sides were losing. It wasn't a situation where anyone could—or would—win.'

'Why did she listen to you?'

'I'm an Elemental. She is educated. Learned in the ancient ways. She recognised what I am. That opened a small window to talk.'

'And that helped?'

'Yes, enough to stop most of the fighting. The territory was split into the domains you see today. The final meetings were in the clearing where you told Metisse and Gabriel who you are. Of course there were skirmishes, but they were squashed. Ishmael and Charmaine made sure of that.'

'My father? He changed his mind?'

'Yes, he did. Charmaine helped him understand.'

'And you.'

He smiled. 'And me.'

'How long ago was this?'

'About a hundred and sixty years ago.' He closed his eyes and I saw the rapid movement indicating he was reliving the scenes of long ago.

'That wasn't it. Was it?' Something else had pushed the enmity to the background. Shivers ran up and down my spine.

'The Council,' Ash confirmed what I already suspected.

'The Sabres had another, more pressing enemy. The Council had found them again.'

'That was how you managed to convince them to stop fighting.' Things were falling into place now.

Again he smiled. He looked so happy with himself when I joined all the dots. Like a doting father or teacher.

'It was,' he continued his narrative. 'I pointed out the real danger was what forced them to flee to our woods in the first place. And sure enough, within three years they were attacked themselves by the Council's assassin's.'

'Was that when Charmaine was wounded?'

'It was.'

'When you saved her?'

'Yes.'

'So your connection with Charmaine started before she was wounded, but was cemented by what happened that day.' He nodded.

Something else nagged at the back of my mind. 'What was Cantix's role in all this?'

'He was an upcoming young wizard then. Very strong and extremely ambitious. He led the assassin team, and through magic and deceit of his own, lured the clan into an ambush. He targeted Charmaine directly when he recognised her as the main threat to the Council. The attack was sudden and brutal. The clan wasn't prepared. Not against Cantix's dark magic. He camouflaged the assassin's with magic. They were upon the clan before the guards noticed, and many of the clan members were killed in the first minutes of the battle. They had been blissfully unaware of the danger so close to them.'

'How did you know?' I asked.

'The magic,' he stated. 'I felt it in the air.'

'You were on time to save Charmaine.'

'Only just. I rushed to the battle, with your father and some of the Wolves in tow. The scene that faced us was terrible. Many dead, from both sides and Cantix about to deliver the killing blow to Charmaine. I intervened.'

That was so Ash, "he intervened". He wouldn't tell me exactly how, I knew that by the way he closed off that avenue with those simple words. I smiled internally. I guess I'd find out one way or the other. Just not now. He didn't think it was important. Need to know.

'Cantix escaped. And I moved to Charmaine. His magic was poisoning her. I managed to stop the process, but it left her a cripple.'

'Yet the Clan kept her as their leader.'

'They did. It was tantamount to the kind of leader she was. Despite her handicap she was—and still is—the strongest Sabre in the Clan. There is no one who will question that.'

No, I guess there wouldn't be. She definitely is one of the strongest person I know. Charmaine and Ash both.

'And Stephan?' I hadn't forgotten him.

'He was incensed Ismael led the Wolves to the Sabre's rescue and that I saved the Sabre leader. He had never forgiven them for the massacre, and Charmaine in particular, though that wasn't really fair. My intervention was viewed as a betrayal by him and his pack, as was Ismael's. They left and set up a new territory in what was then the new emerging big city of Chicago. He's never forgiven me for that.'

'I noticed.'

We sat in silence for a while as I digested everything he had told me.

'Thanks Ash.' He nodded. 'It explains a lot.'

A warm glow spread out from my chest.

'Is that when my father met my mother?'

'Shortly after that. Embre came down to help out while Charmaine was recovering. She initially wanted nothing to do with the Wolves. The age old hostility between the Wolves and Sabres was still fresh in her mind. The animosity dissipated when she got to know Ishmael better.'

'They found each other.'

He nodded. His smile warm.

The circle was complete again. It was back to me and the here and now.

Chapter Thirteen

'There's a guy looking for you.' Gabriel said. This wasn't entirely strange. Many people came looking for me now the word was out.

I nodded, not really paying all that much attention. I has a lot on my mind those days. And none of it is fun. This was not what I'd planned for my life. I think I mentioned that.

'This one is creepy,' he continued. That surprised me. Not as much that a creepy guy was here, we had more than our share of those, but that he unnerved Gabriel.

'How so?'

'He's tiny and skinny, sick, dead nearly, looks like he'll break.'

Yeah, well just about everyone looked skinny compared with the pack members. It's a relative thing.

'The left side of his face looks like it melted.'

That sparked my curiosity.

'Like he was in some kind of fire.'

'He's a wizard,' Metisse chimed in. He looked a bit less freaked-out, though not by much.

A niggling feeling started at the back of my mind. No it couldn't be.

'Did he give a name?' I asked apprehensively.

'Alex.'

'Alex?' Now I was surprised. To the maximum. What was he doing here?

'Yeah, he said you knew him.'

That was the understatement of the year. Had to be. We went way back, like last year.

'I do.' I answered. 'Bring him in, but watch him.'

Alex came in to the room. He looked as mangy as he had six months ago, actually even worse. And now half of his face and his left hand—which he held in a very unnatural position against his body—were covered in horrific burns. They looked raw, painful.

Goosebumps started to form on my arms. I never contemplated we would ever meet again after that memorable last time when he found out what I was. I predicted then he had zero chance of outliving his last report to the council. Yet here he was. Looking for me. That had to be the weirdest thing ever.

Okay, weirdest thing this week.

There was something else different about him. I couldn't put my finger on it as I closely observed him from two metres away where Gabriel told him to stand.

He looked at me. The left side of his face was just as Gabriel described. Like it was melted putty. The left eye socket was empty and about two or three centimetres lower than the one on the right. His lips drooped towards his chin on the left side and gave him a very lopsided and mirthless grin. But there was more. Something I was missing.

Then it hit me.

The nervousness that characterised him when I saw him last, was gone. He stared me straight in the eye and never wavered. His one remaining eye held mine. There was arrogance there, steadfastness, strength. Characteristics that were painfully absent in him before. He dared me to say something.

'You're about the last person I expected to see here.' I finally broke the strained silence.

'I'll bet,' he answered, his tone full of contempt. The stutter was gone. His voice sounded stronger. The words were clear and unwavering.

He refrained from explaining anything else. Okay, so that was the game here. I would have to pull it out of him. He obviously wanted to be in control. Or at least have that perception. I was so astonished he had shown himself here —to me—that I decided to humour him.

'So, why are you here?'

'You owe me.' He was steadfast and locked eyes with me while he made what I could only call his demands.

'How do you figure that?'

'You set me up. Used me as your messenger.' True, but then again he was spying on me, so what did he expect? Alex was seriously naive. He still lived in his own strange world.

'What did you expect?'

'Not this.' He indicated his melted face. It was eerie. No, I guess he wouldn't have.

'What happened?'

'The bitch did this to me.' He didn't have to explain who; Aquanaris.

'So how come she didn't kill you?' It sounded cold, even to me. But this was the question that was foremost in my mind. It was what rang all the bells. By any reckoning, he should be dead. Cantix didn't go easy on messengers. I've seen it before. The giant was vicious, sadistic. He commonly vented his rage on whoever was stupid enough to be near, or the one unlucky soul that brought him the bad news.

'She did.'

I cocked my head in question.

'This,' he waved his right hand over the left side of his body and face. 'This is killing me. It creeps further every day.'

'Looks painful.'

'It is. Beyond compare. But it also fuels my anger.'

I couldn't stop myself from asking, 'why did she do this instead of killing you?'

'Because it was more fun for her. For Cantix. They laughed while I squirmed on the floor. Later she visited me in the infirmary to make sure the poison was progressing through my body. This is the result of disappointing the Council.'

'This is because I sent you back.' I felt a distinct guilt creep up. That was new for me. I never felt remorse about my actions, especially not ones against enemies. It was, I guess, a survival tactic. Everything for the cause. First my personal revenge, now the demise of the Council.

'I didn't have to go back.' Alex brought me back from my reverie. 'I could have disappeared and taken your secret with me. I decided to do my duty, hoping against my better judgement they would not take it out on me. Of course they did. They made me pay for not finding out earlier.' His words were hard, the tone one of a man bent on revenge.

'You blame me?'

'Yes. But, I blame them more.' He was hauntingly frank. The change in him was much, much deeper than the surface, deeper even than the change in his personality. His very reason for existence, his allegiance, his loyalty, all had shifted dramatically.

The question was whether I went for it. Did I believe him? Could I believe someone could change so much? Down to every cell of his body?

'Why should I trust you?'

'You have no reason to.' He laughed coldly. 'And I have no reason to trust you, not after how you treated me.'

That hit a chord with me.

'There was no need for you to treat me the way you did. Sure, I was a spy. We both knew that when we started out. But the contempt with which you approached me was excessive. Needless to say, I resented you for that. Still do. I will go to my grave harbouring that animosity towards you. But you're not the one killing me. They are. The Council. I hate them more than I hate you.'

Wow. That was fierce.

'What do you want?'

'Revenge.'

One word that came from the absolute depth of his soul. His face lit up with the mere mention, his one remaining eye glinted, the right edge of his mouth pulled up in a mockery of a smile.

'I'm dead. There's no way to stop what is happening to me. I will die soon in a horrible manner. I want to go in the knowledge that I helped bring the Council down.'

'And how would you do that?' Metisse asked in disdain. As usual, he wore his opinions on his sleeve. From his height; more than head and shoulders above Alex, he looked down on what he saw as a miserable piece of shit.

I could see where he was coming from. Alex did look

like a homeless person. A begger even. In Metisse's world that was the bottom of the ladder.

If not for the fire that burned in his eye. He barely glanced at Metisee, clearly not here for him.

'I have information about the Council. And talents. Ones that you need.' He looked at me again. 'I can run rings around any one of your computer geeks even with one hand and one eye. And you know it.'

I nodded. He could.

'You're a spy. As you said; what makes you think I'll trust you?'

'You won't.' Again the cold chuckle. 'I wouldn't. You'll just have to decide whether what I can offer is worth the risk. And if not, then kill me. Even that would be a bonus to the long lingering death that awaits me now. It's a win-win situation for me whichever outcome you choose. What you need to think about is what benefit I could be to you and your "cause".'

He spat out the last word. Not a fan I guess.

The matter-of-fact way he spoke of his demise got to me. He had resigned himself to the inevitable. Even to the terrible pain that was definitely in the future. All he lived for now was revenge.

I could understand that. I knew all about living with that one goal. But still, I had the nagging feeling I couldn't just switch around and trust him all of a sudden. This reeked of another of Aquanaris' scams. How the hell would I know if he was genuine? I had to concede that if it was a scam, it was a very elaborate one. One that caused him a lot of discomfort. So either he was legit, or he was extremely loyal to the Council. I would need more info.

I glanced to the right at the shadows where I knew Ash stood. My sensitive eyes saw him leaning against the wall—

as usual—a small smile on his lips as he watched the proceedings unfold.

Ash stood up straight and moved out of the dark into the light. Alex turned his face to see who was coming up on his blind side. His breath stopped as he saw Ash. His one eye opened up to the max and for a moment I saw the old Alex back. Then he regained his composure and stared back at the Shaman. A wry smile pulled the right side of his mouth up a fraction. He slowly shook his head in recognition, then he looked at me.

'I should have known,' he said. I had no idea what he was talking about. He obviously recognised Ash. Or thought he did.

'You've met before?' I asked.

'Yes, we have.'

No further explanation was given by either of them. Ash bridged the distance with six of his large paces. He walked up behind Alex, who cringed slightly. His one eye followed Ash as long as he could while he refused to turn his face.

I had no idea what Ash would do. And I realised for the umpteenth time that there was precious little I knew about the Shaman. I trusted him explicitly. Though I had no idea how he would convince me Alex was legit. The tick that was barely visible in Alex's right eye showed me he did.

Ash took up position behind the much smaller man and lifted his hands until they were parallel to Alex's face. Alex squinted his eye socket shut. The effect was strange with one eye a lot higher that the other. His brow creased from the left under, to the right upper point, pulling the burnt skin on his crown tight and highlighting the ugly red welts and veins.

They looked raw and painful.

'You ready?' Ash asked in a calm voice. 'I'll try to be

gentle.' Alex nodded hesitantly, squeezing his eyes shut even more. Carefully Ash moved his hands closer to Alex until they made contact with his skin. He delicately wrapped his long fingers around the side of Alex's face. There was no sounds in the room, no one moved, everyone rooted to the spot.

I watched in awe.

There was a light blue haze around the two of them. Small sky blue bolts of static electricity crackled around Alex's head. They didn't seem to actually touch him, just swirled around about two centimetres from his skin. I looked up from the mesmerising haze to Ash. The colours in his eyes were bright and mostly blue or purple. The strain he was under showed in the way he creased his forehead and the tightness of his lips. He closed his eyes and I immediately missed the comfort of the colours.

Slowly Alex's tormented face relaxed. His shoulders lowered back to their normal level and the left hand he gripped so desperately slowly dropped down to his side. The incessant movement of his eye under the closed lid diminished and finally stopped. His lips parted slightly and his breathing became regular and deep.

The exact opposite happened with Ash. Drops of perspiration dripped from his brow down his cheeks to the jawline. His forehead creased in concentration and behind his closed eyelids I saw rapid movement. The fingers of his hands were white with the strain. The static electricity became hectic. Moving all around Alex's head and up Ash's arms.

Ash finally lowered his arms and stepped back after what seemed like an eternity. Alex looked almost sorry the link was broken. His eye flicked open. The red rims that characterised it before were softer and less prominent. Tears hung at the edge of his eyelid. He blinked and they slid down his cheek.

I looked past Alex to Ash. His head was bowed, looking at his hands. He looked up at me and we locked eyes. The swirling of colours I was so used to was still there, only now the tints were dark and foreboding. They'd taken over the whole surface of his eyes, pushing the white away. Pearls of sweat still dripped down his face.

I cocked my head in a silent question whether he was alright. He nodded slowly. Then more pronounced. He was okay. Slowly his eyes became softer again and I saw my friend and mentor return to his normal self.

Ash moved to the side, away from Alex who remained where he was with an almost blissful look on his face.

I turned back to my friend, he nodded again. Now about Alex. He was genuine. I would need to talk to the Shaman later to find out exactly what he learned from Alex's mind. For now, his validation was enough.

Gabriel stood next to me. 'Could you please find somewhere for Alex to stay?' I asked. 'He will need to rest I expect.'

Gabriel nodded, signalled to Alex to follow him and they left the room.

We would need to discuss the difference Alex's presence would make to our plans. He had inside knowledge of our enemies.

That could be a game changer.

Chapter Fourteen

'What happened in there?' Ash looked at me and contemplated his answer.

'With Alex?'

I nodded. Ash's demeanour changed profoundly when he read Alex's mind, not to mention the colour of his eyes; a definite give-away of his mood.

The campfire warmed my face in the cool evening air as I waited for him to continue.

The ring of rocks and logs around the fire was a favourite place for me to unwind at the end of a long day. I mused over how my life had changed in the past months. Earlier I enjoyed comforts like a good hotel room, my own house in California and watching films. Now, it's the open air, good friends and the heat of the flames.

'His mind is in chaos.' Ash continued as I stared into the flames. 'Understandably, there is a lot of anger.'

'At me?'

'Some of it, though not much really. The majority of the resentment is aimed at the Council in general, and

Cantix and Aquanaris in particular. They really did a number on the poor guy.' He sighed audibly. 'He was right. He is dying.'

'But you stopped it?' The almost serene look on Alex's face after the contact with Ash gave me the idea the Shaman had intervened in whatever Aquanaris put in Alex's body.

He shook his head slowly and his lips tightened. 'Not stopped,' he said softly. 'I just gave him some relief. He's too far gone for me to really make a difference. If he'd arrived here earlier, I might have been able to maybe not cure him, but at least stop the progress of the poison. Now I can only give him relief.'

He stared into the fire, the reflection of the flames shone in his eyes. The only sound was the crackling of the fire and a distant wolf howl. Someone was hunting. I recognised the tone and pitch. It was Gabriel's beta.

'What exactly is it?' I asked carefully.

Ash turned his head to me and smiled, his concentration on the flames broken. I would love to know where his mind went to at times like this. Far away, I guess.

'It's a magical poison, very much like the one Cantix used to attack Charmaine. In Alex's case it turns his blood against him. Parts of his body are being digested by his own bodily fluids. It creeps through the veins and eats away at his very existence. I've slowed its progress and numbed the pain. He can't feel the degradation as much as he could.'

'How long does he have?'

'Not long. The poison hasn't reached many of his vital organs yet, but it is just a matter of time.' I cocked my head in question, more details please. 'I think a month or two. It will not be pleasant. I can alleviate the pain a bit as long as he is here. But no more than that.'

I sighed.

Sure, I'd been a bitch while Alex was tasked with watching me, and I didn't particularly like the guy. But this was cruel. Sadistic. No one should go through this. I wouldn't wish this on my worst enemy. Well, maybe I would on whoever killed my mother. Not on Alex though. I understood his resentment.

'Actually the pain and imminent death is not what angers him most,' Ash answered my unspoken questions. The uncanny way he knew exactly what I was thinking made me wonder whether he had found a way into my thoughts. It might be childish of me, but I still wouldn't let him into my inner thoughts. I trust him with my life. Just not with my thoughts. They are mine. And that's the way they'll stay. It's nonsensical and stubborn, I know. But hey, that's me.

I urged him on.

'Alex never had an easy life,' that I could imagine.

'The guy was a bully magnet. His whole demeanour screamed at people to put him down, pester him, bully him.'

'I delved into his memories and found his earliest recollections. He's been harassed and oppressed ever since his wretched childhood. It made him wary of direct contact with others and as so often happens; he lost himself in technology. His magic skills are surprisingly good, though he trusts his computers more than his paranormal abilities. I expect because they are more constant and predictable.'

'His magic was one of the reasons he was persecuted as a child. Always the wall flower, the outcast, he was recruited by the Council in his late teens. That gave him the family he never had. It gave him a purpose. Formed him. He wanted to be a picture-perfect employee. His need to make his new family proud was so extreme he closed his mind to what the

Council did. He wanted to belong. They gave him his value. His reason for living.'

'He's good at anything to do with computers.' I chimed in, my memory turning back to the time we arrived in Weisland.

'Alex's whole being is centred around loyalty, around his new family. He was fiercely devoted to the Council and the paranormal society. He basked in the feeling of value and home that they gave him. Something he hunkered for as a child and adolescent.'

'And now that has been betrayed.' I started to understand.

Ash nodded. There was sadness in his face. He picked up a log next to the rock he sat on and placed it carefully on the now dimming fire. Then another, and another. He waved his hand over the new tinder that immediately caught fire and blazed; warming us.

Magic is soooo handy.

'The treachery eats away at him as much as the poison.' Ash continued. 'It fuels his hatred. His extreme loyalty to the Council has done a full one-eighty. He is determined to see Cantix fall. Alex is single-minded in his ambitions. He will not stop at wounding the Council. He wants it destroyed. Obliterated. He wants Cantix and Aquanaris dead.'

'So we can trust him?'

'As long as our goals are in line with his, yes. But you need to be careful. The poison will continue to ravish his body, it could attack his brain and his paranormal abilities in ways that we are not yet aware.'

'Can you keep an eye on him?'

'Yes. He will need me to relieve the pain on a regular basis. For that I need access to his mind. I will monitor the progress of the degeneration and the effect on his psyche.'

Silence descended on the clearing. We both lost ourselves in our own thoughts. The flames danced and crackled on the logs and hypnotised me with their colours and warmth. I found myself descending more and more into memories of my mother. Images resurfaced of woodland fire places where we warmed ourselves while on the run for the Council. The cold on my back reminded me of the many days and nights body heat was our only fuel. The fur of our feline bodies saved us through those hard times.

The Council.

That body of power determined my life from the earliest possible recollection. As soon as I set foot in this world my future was intertwined with that of the Council and its members. There would be no peace for me until the connection was gone. My destiny was to bring them down. I would. There was no doubt, at least not in my mind. Alex and I shared a goal. I could use his talents. Both technical and maybe even magical. At least for now; we would be allies.

'There was something else.' Ash's words brought me back to the present. My right eyebrow raised and my brow scrunched in question.

'Deep in his memories I saw a thread I followed.'

Goosebumps started at the bottom of my spine and slowly made their way up my back to raise the hairs on the back of my neck. A slow ache started at the back of my skull and pushed at my consciousness. I sat back on the rock and stared at Ash, apprehensive of what he might say. The intensity of his gaze burned a hole in my mind. The kaleidoscope of colours in the irises were swirling too quickly to calm me. They hypnotised me, as they always do, but the result—the serenity it usually brought me—was absent.

I had tingles all over.

'What did you see?' Gabriel sat down next to me on the rock as he asked the question. I moved over a bit to give him enough room.

Metisse took a place on one of the big logs opposite us on the other side of the fire. I was so lost in my thoughts that I hadn't heard them approach.

That was not like me. My instincts ruled my mind and were constantly in a state of high alert. I'd been so immersed in my memories and the pain they caused, I ignored my instincts. That or the feeling of security was so overwhelming here it prevented my alarms from going off. Okay, these were my soulmates, so no danger there. But still. I would have to watch myself. I need to be on high alert. We all do. The Council could be out there.

Gabriel felt my unease and took my hand in his, softly stroking my fingers. Across the fire Metisse flinched almost imperceptibly. He took a deep breath and forcibly relaxed his shoulders, stretching his fingers out of the closed fists. The only giveaway was the blazing of his eyes. I'd have to speak to him again tonight. These two were driving me mad with their rivalry.

Ash's gaze went to both of my mates. He smiled at me and leaned forward, his elbows on his knees as he cleared his throat.

He seemed almost nervous. That was a trait I never expected to see in the big man. My stomach turned. He was my rock, how could he be nervous? A feeling of dread filled my body. What could be that bad so that he was hesitant to share.

'In one of his memories,' he finally began. 'I saw something he worked on for the Council. A long time ago. Decades.'

I was so thankful for Gabriel's hand in mine and from the edge of my eye I saw Metisse stand up and move to my side of the fire. He took up a position on the other side of me from Gabriel, and his hand squeezed my shoulder in support. My hand covered his in gratitude, and I smiled up at him. It was a strained smile I couldn't keep for very long. I forced myself to stay seated and not rush over and shake Ash. I needed to know, even if I dreaded what he might say. The skin on the back of my hands tingled as fur came through.

'He was involved in the hunt for you and Embre.' The silence could be cut with a knife. Just when I'd convinced myself that Alex wasn't all bad, Ash sprung another reason on me to hate the guy.

'How?' I whispered. Gabriel's hand felt hot in mine, like the fingers of Metisse as they softly stroked my shoulder. The world ceased to exist around me. All I could do was focus on the Shaman. Everything else was a blur. My heart-beat pounded in my ears, drowning out any woodland sounds.

'He did some of the research,' Ash continued, his voice almost as quiet as me. 'He trolled both internets to find any mention of a lone Sabre with a child.'

'And he found us.' It wasn't really a question.

Ash nodded. His head went up and down in slow motion as everything came to a standstill. Alex was the one who found us. He pointed the dragon to where we were.

'He is not to blame for what happened after that, Trish.' Ash tried.

I disagreed. He found us. Alex did. That made him an accomplice. Or more. Without him she might still be alive.

My blood heated and fur pushed through on all of my limbs. Soft amber fur of the Sabre, alternated with the course canine hair of the black wolf. The waves of change unnerved Metisse and he squeezed my shoulder harder. Gabriel continued to stroke my hand as it morphed into a paw, then back to human again.

'Alex only found you. The council attacked your mother, not him.'

How could he protect Alex? Didn't he realise the impact his words would have on me? Of course he did. Still he continued.

'There is more.'

'More?' I shouted. My anger filled me like a tsunami. I felt the rage move up from my body through my neck to my head.

'Yes. There is more. The Council sent the dragon and a cadre of wizards to apprehend you and Embre.'

I stared at him.

'They were ordered to bring you in alive, both of you.'

'They didn't. They killed her.' I screamed out my anguish. Metisse knelt down beside me and tried to pull me close. I resisted. I didn't want comfort. I wanted blood.

'They didn't.'

My eyes opened to their maximum. I stopped breathing as I stared at Ash. They didn't? What did he mean? They didn't kill her? How was that possible?

'They brought Embre back alive,' he continued.

'No,' I whispered. 'There was too much blood. She was dead.'

'She was wounded. Badly. But the dragon brought her back to the Council where Aquanaris tended to her.'

Realisation hit me like a hammer. I recoiled visibly. 'She's alive?'

'I don't know.' His eyes were once again soothing, the colours muted and soft. The creases in his brow showed me how difficult it was for Ash to tell me this.

'You knew.' Understanding flowed over me.

'I suspected,' he answered.

'You suspected what?' Gabriel asked.

'That Embre might not have died that day. There have been rumours. There always are.'

'In the clearing,' I said in a daze. 'The day we all came together. That was what you almost told me.'

He nodded.

'Why didn't you tell her earlier?' Metisse's tone was hard.

'I needed more proof. The impact would be too great if I was wrong.' Ash was oblivious to the resentment in Metisse's words.

I nodded. About what, I didn't know anymore. My anger dissipated like snow in the sun. A hollow feeling of utter agony filled the void of where the rage had just been. Tears flowed from my eyes. Gabriel's hands covered my own and stopped the shaking that racked me.

My mother didn't die on that fateful day. She might be alive now. Somewhere.

'We have to find her.' My words were hardly audible.

'If she is still alive,' Ash added carefully. 'The memories I picked out of Alex's mind are from very long ago. I couldn't find what happened to her after the seer healed her.'

'He doesn't know?' Gabriel asked.

'He might. I would need to go deeper into his mind to find out. I can't do that without him knowing and permitting the search.'

'Then we have to force him to let you.' Metisse exclaimed.

'No,' I interrupted. 'We have to ask him. We can't force him.'

Ash nodded his approval.

Silence filled the area. Only our breathing was audible. It was as though Nature was holding its breath, like me.

'I need a drink.' Trust Ash to break the tension.

Metisse stared at him in disbelief, Gabriel smiled.

I laughed. 'We all need a drink.'

Okay, everyone agreed on that. 'Maybe more than one.' More nods. 'Then we need to make plans.'

Our quest had just taken on a completely new dimension.

Chapter Fifteen

So now I was dependent on Alex. Not a place I wanted to be. But, it was exactly where I was. There was no escaping that. Bummer.

I paced the room. 'Why would he help me? I mean, I wasn't really nice to him before.' Gabriel raised his eyebrows in question. 'Okay, I was a complete shit-head.'

'He will.' Gabe was so optimistic.

'Why would he?' My thoughts were a lot darker. 'I wouldn't.'

'Because of Ash.'

Well, at least he wasn't pulling any punches. He was right though. If—and that's a very big "IF"—Alex chose to help find my mother it would be because Ash could help him manage the debilitating pain. I had no illusions about his feelings for me, no matter what Ash says.

'And otherwise we'll force him.' Metisse interrupted my thoughts. Trust Metisse to revert to blunt force.

Both my lovers were with me in the living room of my

house in a rare moment of togetherness. They were each acutely aware of the importance of this meeting.

'That won't work,' I answered him. 'You heard Ash yesterday, he needs Alex's cooperation.'

Metisse hated it when I disagreed with him, especially when Gabriel was around. His lips started to pout and he forced the breath through his nose in an irritated huff. Gabriel smiled; almost laughed at the childishness of his romantic rival. That earned him a dark stare from Metisse, which in turn only expanded the smile.

'Can it, guys.' I interrupted. 'I have no time for your stupid adolescent games now.' They were once again getting on my nerves. I wanted to bash their heads together at times, and this was one of them. I had no patience for their petty games. Not now. Not when I had to figure out how I could convince Alex.

The door opened and Ash's massive frame filled the doorway. The door was higher than normal height, but he still needed to duck to come in. There was a big smile on his face as he walked over to me and kissed the top of my head, as was his custom.

It gave me conflicting emotions as usual. On the one side it made me feel safe, on the other; slightly patronised. He even had to bend his head to reach the top of mine. He made me feel small. I think he enjoyed the duplicity. I asked him once why he did it, he just smiled and said it made him happy.

Behind him, Alex stopped in the doorframe. His head moved to the left, then the right, as he took in the living room and its occupants, his one eye roamed over us all. Shivers went up and down my spine. I nodded to him. He nodded back. Okay, we were at least on civil terms.

'Please, sit down.' I tried to convey welcome in my tone.

Ash took his pre-offered seat in the reclining chair, Alex settled on the edge of the sofa, as far away from Metisse as possible. It placed him opposite me.

'Coffee anyone?' Gabriel broke the heavy silence.

'Please.' Ash answered light-heartedly.

Alex nodded, like Metisse and me. Gabe left the seating area and made his way to the open kitchen and the coffee-maker.

I watched him leave, jealous I couldn't just escape the uncomfortable situation as well. But it wasn't an option. This was necessary. I took a deep breath and let the action itself calm me, at least outwardly.

'Thanks for coming, Alex,' I started off, hoping I sounded sincere.

He turned his one eye to me and observed my face.

I felt scrutinised; not a nice feeling. The old Alex was nothing like the one sitting opposite me now. This one sat up straight, his good arm on the arm rest of the sofa. The other in his lap, the wrist curled painfully tight into a ball. His one eye glinted in the light that shone through the big windows. The shadows cast by the heavy eyebrows and hooked nose emaciated his face even more. The grey mottled skin with bright red welts didn't help either. His lips were tight; the creases at the sides exaggerated by the tension.

He didn't react. Just waited for me to tell him why he was here. Well, here goes nothing.

'I have a favour to ask.' Again no reaction. My hands felt clammy, my shirt stuck to my back from the perspiration.

Get a grip girl!

I took another deep breath and just went for it. 'Yesterday, when Ash read your mind he saw something.'

Alex glanced at the ever smiling Ash. '

He saw a memory of a job you did for the Council.'

Again, Alex glanced at the big man. I could not read anything off his face and that irritated me. He was blank. Nothing.

'You helped them to hunt down a Sabre woman and her child.'

He cocked his head and raised his brow in what I hoped was recollection.

'Decades ago.' Still no reply. It was my turn now to look at Ash. He just blinked and urged me wordlessly to continue.

'They sent a dragon and the woman was caught.' The words stuck in my throat. I tried to keep it all very emotionless, but it wasn't working. This was my mother we were talking about. My Mother! Alex was involved in what happened that day. Maybe not directly, but he made it possible.

'Why would I help you? This has nothing to do with the fight we're in now. It's irrelevant.' He aimed a dark look at Ash. Presumably for picking it out of his mind.

My heart sank. He was completely right.

'It is the start of all of this,' I tried to convince him. 'That woman was my mother. The Council was looking for her—for me—because of the prophecy.'

'The prophecy is what brings everyone here. What's amassing our army. Without Trish, there would be no fight. No revolution.' Gabriel chimed in.

'I have no right to demand answers from you,' I continued haltingly, as I desperately tried to reign in my emotions. 'I know that. All I can do is ask. I don't know what happened to her that day. Just that she was taken from me. There was so much blood I presumed she died that day.

The Council ripped my only family away from me. They made me an orphan. I was twelve years old and alone. Please, I need to know. Anything that you remember. Even the smallest thing. She was my mother.'

I wanted to shake him. Hit him. Force him to tell me all he knew. Anything to get to the information stored in the recesses of his brain. I couldn't function without knowing what happened. In the past hours, all I'd been able to think of was my mother and that fateful day in the maize field. My nerves were frayed and I was ready to attack anything and anyone.

'Embre.' Alex's voice brought me back from my inner rantings and I stared at him. He knew her name. He remembered. Ash came to Alex's rescue just before I pounced on him.

'Yes, Alex. Embre.'

I just stared at Ash, then back to Alex. I was rapidly losing the battle to stay calm and reserved. Now the sadness and utter loneliness swamped me. The pinpricks behind my eyes heralded the tear drops I knew would follow. The bile in my throat wouldn't go down as I tried to swallow. There was a numbness in my head that made everything seem slow-motion. I could see the surprise on Gabriel's face too. He stared at me.

'You remember.' I said softly.

'I remember every job I did for the Council.' Disdain dipped off Alex's words. How could I have doubted him? Yeah, well my feelings run deep.

'What do you remember about this one?' Ash intervened. I was relieved he took over, my emotions were all over the place. Metisse noticed and moved closer.

'Everything.' Alex answered Ash curtly. 'I remember everything. All of the assignments. Every lie Cantix told me.

Every manipulation that bitch did.' We all stayed quiet. No one dared to speak.

Alex's voice was surprisingly clear and strong.

This particular one was ninety years ago. I was tasked with trolling both the regular and the paranormal internet in search of any mention of a strong warrior woman with a child. I didn't know if it was a girl or a boy, but that didn't matter. I had a name: Embre. It's not a common name and so when it came up it stood out. She used other names, but there were many people who knew her by her real name. She was a person of standing within the paranormal society.'

I remembered. We changed our names every time we moved. All trails of the person we had been were discarded and we started anew. Again and again.

'It took more than six months, but I finally found a small clue. Then a break when someone betrayed her.'

Betrayed her?

He continued, 'I followed the thread, watched it develop. She was moving slowly in a roundabout manner to Weisland. Like she was scouting the place, and maybe also hiding from the occupants. It was a bold choice. There were a lot of potential helpers, but also many people who would recognise her as the Sabre chief the Council was searching for. She was clever. Never stayed in one place long enough to cause any suspicion. Just not clever enough. Someone greedy called us.'

'What happened?' I was so grateful Ash asked the questions I couldn't get over my lips.

'Cantix sent a cadre after her, her and the kid.' He looked at me. 'You?'

I nodded, riveted to my seat. I felt Metisse slide on to the cushion next to me. He put his arm around my shoulders and I was glad for the warmth he provided. I felt cold. Shivered even. Dread sent its icy tentacles through my veins.

'And a dragon,' Alex added. 'The orders were to bring them both back alive.'

'Alive?' I stammered.

'Yeah. Cantix and that bitch of his wanted to study the Lamaq. They figured it would be easier with the mother there. Either to help, or to use as a hostage.'

I closed my eyes. It didn't help. Against the inside of my eyelids, I saw the replay of that fateful day. Every detail of the blue sky, the high vegetation we ran through and most of all the bellowing of the dragon. All was securely grafted into my mind and soul.

'They came back with Embre. Not you. They lost you.' Alex aimed his words at me. There was a softness in his tone I hadn't heard before. I opened my eyes and blinked the tears away.

'She was alive when they brought her to Cantix?'

'Yes. Though barely. She fought valiantly. Her courage was what let you escape. The cadre desperately searched for you, but you'd disappeared.' My memory returned to the embankment where I hid that fateful day, the ferns and leaves covering me and shielding any scent.

'They brought Embre to the Council?' Ash prompted Alex to continue.

'Yes. To Aquanaris. She healed her. Embre was a prisoner for a long time. They—Cantix and the bitch—tried to force her to help them search for you. She never said a word. Never let on to anything. Not even your name.' There was admiration in his voice. 'By then, we knew the child was female, but no more than that. That continued for decades. Finally they gave up and sent her to Alaska to the paranormal high security compound.'

'What happened to her after that?'

'I don't know. Not for sure. I tried to keep up to date on what her status was. She intrigued me. Her courage and single-mindedness. I admired her for it. Even though, at the time, I thought she was misguided. I know now that she wasn't. She saw what we all didn't want to believe. That our paranormal world is ruled by a tyrant.'

He paused to pick up his coffee and slowly drank a few sips. Even that was a chore for him because the left side of his face was ravaged and lopsided. Balancing the lip of the cup on his mouth was difficult. We waited for him to continue.

'I heard things, every now and then. She escaped, went underground for a few months, but was caught again later. I didn't find her that time. The Council had others search for her. I didn't want to enslave her again. She earned her freedom in my opinion.' He sounded sincere.

'She's alive?' My voice was hardly eligible. I daren't say it out loud, scared of his answer, that it might not be true.

'I'm not sure. I never found any mention of her death. That's all I know. She could be.'

'If she was still a prisoner,' Gabriel voiced my questions. 'Where would she be?'

'Not in Alaska. She escaped from there. There are other places. Clandestine, even for the Council. These are locations where Cantix and Aquanaris send their most important prisoners. Ones they do not want in close contact with Council members. Embre never made her opinion about Cantix and the Council a secret. She openly accused both Cantix and the seer of genocide and murder, and the Council of negligence. Despite the status of fugitive, she still had a lot of respect and authority in the paranormal world.

There were also many who hoped the prophecy would one day become reality.'

'But you know where they are.' Metisee stated resolutely. 'The prisons?'

'Yes, I do.' Alex looked at Ash and then to me. His gaze bored into my soul.

'I'll help you,' he finally said, allowing me to breath again. 'Not because you ask. Because of her. Her audacity in the face of Cantix. Her fearlessness and undying love for you. That's why I'll help.'

'I can't promise she's still alive. I don't know,' he added.

I nodded my thanks. 'It would give closure at the very least,' he added.

My world had just been turned upside down.

There was a distinct possibility my mother was still alive. We might find her. I wasn't an orphan after all.

It was overwhelming.

Chapter Sixteen

'When are we finally going to war?' Stephan voiced what others were thinking. Up to now, we had been reactive. The main objective was to grow our numbers and protect those who came to us. Which in itself was quite a challenge. But the people joined to overthrow the Council. They expected a war. They expected a strategy. A plan.

Yeah, I wanted one of those too.

What the hell was I going to do. I'm not a strategist. Not by a million miles.

'Follow your instinct,' Ash said in his normal evasive manner. 'You are the child of your father and mother. They were excellent leaders.'

Great, crank up the pressure. Thanks Ash. Fuck load of help that was.

Actually, it was. I'm not being fair here. What he did was make me think. He supports me and helps once I've determined a route. But he lets me decide. I guess he has to. This is my prophecy after all.

Sometimes I think he knows how it should be, and at other times I think he's as much in the dark as I am.

Anyway, back to the present. The pack and clan leaders were all gathered in the clearing that had become the communal meeting grounds. Seats were placed in a circle. I flatly refused to sit at the head of anything. It made me feel very exposed. So they all humored me and pretended wherever I am is not the centre of everything.

Who's kidding whom?

Stephan called this meeting. Anyone could do that. It was a democracy here. Kind of.

'We came to fight,' he continued. 'Not to sit on our ass and wait for the Council to pick us off one by one.'

He had a point.

About the fighting.

The Prophecy was interpreted as a war by most of our supporters. I'm not sure that was what Kimi meant when she landed it on the world, but perception was everything, so war it would be. There was also the fact the Council wouldn't listen to reason which made force the only real option.

Now, how to go to war?

Stephan was going on and on about how he wanted to fight, that blood was needed. It was a thing with him. Frankly, he was getting on my nerves.

'What do you suggest?' I asked him in my most friendly voice. Friendly under the circumstances.

'What?' he exclaimed surprised. The Wolf way was to follow orders from the Alpha. Technically that was me. Especially after I bested him. Now I was asking him for advice. He was flustered. I think he honestly had no idea. Hadn't really thought about it. He was completely ready to follow.

'What do you suggest?' I repeated sweetly, secretly enjoying his unease. He shut up and sat down. Finally.

'You're right,' I threw him a bone. 'We are at war.' Lots of nodding all around. 'The Council knows we're here. They try to stop people from joining us. Our forces grow and we need to prepare for battle.'

I remembered what Ash told me. 'The Council will not want a head-on fight. They do not go to war as a strong military force. They try to undermine our unity by biting at the foundation of our coalition. They instigate. Set us against each other. Why? Because they fear our strength and our numbers.'

I took a breath and let the words flow. I glanced at Ash. He nodded slightly and a small smile flitted over his lips. Just long enough for me to see.

'We have the strength. We have the numbers. It's time we made use of them.' That was met by a nervous silence.

'We will bring the fight to the Council.'

Occasional nods. Okay, they were warming to the idea. 'We will eat at the fringes of the Council. Upset their lines of defence. Free their prisoners.'

Now they were seriously cheering. Even Metisse and Gabriel were smiling now.

'We have information on the location of their prisons,' I continued. 'Soon, we will bring the fight to them.'

I could hardly get myself heard over the cheers now. Was that all it took? It seemed so shallow. Not a real plan at all. Just a call to action. I guess that was exactly what they needed at this time.

'We will plan where we hit first and with whom,' I continued once it was finally a bit quieter. Nods again. 'It will be soon.'

'You certainly raised them up to the challenge,' Metisse

said once we were in a smaller group. Ash and Gabriel were still there, along with Metisse and Charmaine.

'Well done, Trish.' Charmaine echoed.

'For what? I didn't really say anything specific.'

'You didn't have to,' Gabriel answered for them all. 'You rallied them around the cause again and gave them a goal. Free the prisoners. That's a great way to get them invested. The Council holds prisoners from most packs and some of the clans. they all stand to profit from this.'

'Yeah, I guess. Now all we have to do is make good on the statement.'

'You're not alone in this, Trish,' Ash reassured me. 'We're here to help you.'

Now I'd decided on the first line of action, I could count on the help of the strategists, thank God for that. But it had to be my decision. Frankly, I had no idea where it had come from. It just seemed right. Maybe I should trust my instincts more.

Who knows. It just might be in the genes.

We decided to mount a recognisance on two of the major prisons to gain even more information than we had now.

Our secret asset: Alex, was a fountain of information. He knew exactly where the prisons were, where the garrisons were located and what their strength was. What he didn't know, he found on the dark paranormal web. There were more than enough people willing to betray the Council, as long as they stayed in the shadows out of danger. Alex knew where to look, who to talk to, and what questions to ask. Me, I was much to straight forward.

'And what do you suggest?' he asked me with that patronising tone that rubbed me the wrong way. He stared at me with his one eye. It made me feel extremely uncomfortable. 'Something like: "Tell me where the prison is." That about it?'

I stayed silent. What was I supposed to say? Alex looked at me as though I was an ignorant child. I felt like one and didn't like the feeling. But he was right. It just about summed up what I wanted to propose.

'These people are nervous. They're scared of the Council, Most of them have experienced the wrath of Cantix and Aquanaris themselves. They know what the price of their betrayal will be, if the witch ever found out. Death would seem like a gift.' His words were emphasised by the ugly welts on his face and the slowly expanding paralysis. And this was just the result of him delivering bad news. He hadn't even betrayed the Council. Not then.

'I have to convince them their words will not come back to haunt them. Persuade them their secret is safe with me. It's no easy feat.'

I nodded. What else could I do.

Alex continued to lecture me on how to approach informants. It was enlightening, but not my thing.

This wasn't my forfait so, after that lesson, I left him to it.

Chapter Seventeen

'You have a mole.' I hated it when Alex did that. He entered the room quietly and just materialised in front of me without a sound. I suspect he did it on purpose. A childish way of getting back at me for all the hassle I put him through earlier. I couldn't blame him really. There was just a hint of a smile for a fleeting moment when I looked up from the documents Metisse and I were studying.

Other than that, Alex's face was emotionless. His one eye blank.

'What?' I exclaimed.

Alex looked at me quizzically, as though he didn't understand my reaction to the revelation he just sprung on me. It was a statement. There was no inflection, no anger, just a proclamation.

The reaction of my companions was quite different to Alex's. Metisse looked up from what he was doing and stared at the one-eyed wizard. Gabriel, standing next to me, cocked his head, his brow creased. Ash unfolded his long body from the low recliner and joined us at the desk.

'A mole?' I asked incredulously. The thought honestly never crossed my mind. A bit naive, I know. But the people I encountered were just so committed to overthrowing the Council I never seriously entertained the idea. Not even after the incident months ago. I also had too much on my mind recently. In hindsight, not such a good idea.

'Please explain, Alex,' Ash took over, very interested. 'Take a seat.' Alex looked around, noticed the three guys looking at him attentively and then stared at the chair Ash pointed to.

He had these kind of moments; when he came up to me so absorbed with what he was going to say he was completely oblivious of anyone else. I guess he was so concentrated on what he had to do, he ignored anything around him.

'I found some references about here. Things I never reported. Subjects they would never know.'

'What kind of things?'

'Things like how many people are here, who just joined. That kind of thing.'

His matter-of-fact way of delivering the news was in stark contrast to the effect it had on me. This was dangerous information in the hands of the Council. No scrap that, we'd passed that point. I shuddered to think of what else they knew.

'Can you trace the source of the information?'

Thank God for Ash, he was at least keeping his wits about him and asking the right questions. I was much more in panic mode. Metisse was just getting very mad and Gabriel mirrored the Shaman in interest.

'No. I can't find the actual messages, just references to them and the information itself.'

'So nothing?' I asked and immediately regretted it. If

there had been a way to follow the message back to whomever had sent it, Alex would have found it. He looked at me and raised his one brow, pulling his face even more crooked. 'Sorry,' I mumbled.

'Is there a way to pinpoint the timing?' Gabriel asked much more relevant questions.

'Only based on the content.' Alex turned towards him. 'The last mention I could find was of the Miami Wolf pack wanting to join the cause. So that's what, a week ago?'

I nodded.

It explained a lot.

The Council seemed to be one step ahead of us all the way. They came down like a brick wall on the Miami pack just two days ago. Many of the pack were either missing or dead. It sent a clear message to any paranormals contemplating rebellion. The survivors had stumbled to Weisland and were now under the protection of Gabriel's pack.

'What else do they know?' I asked.

'A lot.' Alex produced a stack op papers. 'I printed most of what I found. To make it easier for you to read.'

There was a condescending tone to his voice, but I let it pass. There were more important things here; like how do we find the mole?

'Maybe we can piece together what level of information the Council knows and that could point us in the direction of where to look,' Metisse suggested.

It sounded like a good idea. The information was given out on a need-to-know basis. The higher up you got in our small club, the more access you had to sensitive information. I dreaded the outcome. If it was someone in our close group, then that would devastate me. I couldn't think straight. Who would betray us? And why?

It was just too much to handle on top of all I learned in the past weeks.

I took a deep breath and collected my thoughts.

We had to solve this. There was no doubt it could have far-reaching consequences. Not just because of the information the Council received, but also because of repercussions it could have in our strange band of brothers and sisters.

The peace between normally warring paranormal creatures was a tentative and fragile one. Its sole purpose and reason for existence was the fight against the Council. Past differences were put on hold, as were old feuds. The presence of a traitor could be the spark to blow this powder keg of mixed emotions.

'Thank you Alex,' I returned to the here-and-now. 'I don't like the news, but I'm glad you found it.'

He nodded, a very faint hint of a smile pulled the one moveable corner of his mouth up a fraction.

'I'll continue to monitor it,' he proclaimed happily and turned to leave.

'Please keep it under wraps for now, Alex.' I called after him. 'We don't want to cause any panic or a witch hunt.' Turning back, he nodded. Then left the room.

Who would he talk to? Alex was almost a hermit, locked up in that computer room surrounded by monitors. Most of the people here were unaware of his existence. Anyone out of the small inner circle here in the building was blissfully unaware that a former wizard was assisting us.

We were silent. No one wanted to take the first step to find out whom of our friends was betraying us.

'Do you trust him?' Metisse asked. He still had a thing about Alex. I think it was as much due to his own inability to deal with the man's handicaps, as it was real doubts. I looked at Ash.

'He's trustworthy,' the Shaman commented resolutely. Metisse was about to question Ash's conviction but thought better of it and kept his mouth shut.

'I'm in his mind every other day,' Ash explained. 'To numb the pain of his infliction. I see the fire with which he hates Cantix and Aquanaris. I see his resolve. He will not betray us as long as our goals coincide with his. He wants to take them down.'

One down, lots more to go. We had to painstakingly cross everyone off our list.

First the documents. They could help. I reached out for them, but Gabriel beat me to it.

'I'll take a first look,' he offered. My relief must have be obvious, and he smiled. He took the papers and went to the sofa to look through them, Ash joined him. Metisse stayed with me.

'Who do you think?' he asked me after a few minutes of silence.

'I don't have anyone who springs to mind straight away,' I tried.

'Yeah, right.'

'Okay,' I conceded. 'Maybe one.'

'Mariah?' Now it was my turn to nod.

'Do you have any real reason for that other than your mutual dislike?'

He hit the nail on the head. Those were my thoughts exactly. Mariah and I didn't get along. Okay, that's an understatement. We butt heads in the tactical meetings all the time.

'Her resentment towards you would never be enough to allow her to betray her clan.'

I looked up at Metisse. I knew he liked Mariah. And yes,

she was a good second-in-command. But she also harboured a lot of resentment against me and the cause. I had no idea whether it was enough for her to change sides, but then again I didn't know her very well. Metisse did. They grew up together, were even an item for a while. Yet another reason why she hated my guts.

She was extremely arrogant when it came to the Wolves, like Metisse in some ways, and the current situation with many different packs in the same area was not going down well with her.

'What do you think?' I countered.

'She would never endanger the clan,' he answered seriously. 'Her loyalty is without question. To the clan and to my mother. It's not her.'

'Well, we'll see, won't we? When Ash and Gabe come back with their first analysis.'

'I'll go help them,' he offered.

I saw through the helpfulness. He was anxious about what they might find. Maybe he wasn't so sure about Mariah as he made out to be.

Later that evening the guys reported their findings. It was as bad as it could get. Worse than I thought.

'There is very sensitive information in there,' Ash started as my heart sank. 'The strength of our army. Who pledged their allegiance. The basics of some of our plans.'

Anger started to get a hold of my emotions. How could anyone do this?

'Any clear pointers?'

'Not specifically to one person,' he answered carefully.

'A group?' There were times when Ash's avoidance tactics got on my nerves. This was one of them.

'Not a species, but definitely a group.'

I stared at him, willing him to continue, and dreading what he would say.

'The inner circle.' He finally answered.

Shit.

The leaders of the packs and clans. The inner circle was twelve strong. Men and women who had brought their people here, to fight with us, to be safe. And now one of them was leading us all to certain death. Next to the leaders; there were us four, that left eight maybes. Eight people I didn't want it to be.

'The group could be a bit larger,' Gabriel came to my rescue. 'The leaders may have told their own seconds and a few others. We did say to keep everything quiet, but some people in the clans and packs do need to know certain things.'

Okay, a bigger group. Good that it might not be one of the leaders, but the group of suspects just got a lot larger.

'How can we narrow the search?'

'We thought we might spread some fake stories and see when Alex returns one of the subjects. We could do a different subject for each clan or pack. That would at least let us know where exactly to look.' Gabriel seemed hopeful.

'It's a good start,' I answered.

'But?'

'But it will take time. We need to find whoever it is faster.'

'We can do multiple things at the same time.' Ash intervened. 'Start with this and continue to search out who it may be.'

'We have to be careful. No one can know we are investigating anyone.'

They all agreed.

'And no mention can be made of Alex. He's a trump card. One the Council is still not aware of yet. Let's keep it that way.' Again nods. 'Go to sleep and let's reconvene again tomorrow to see what we can do.'

Chapter Eighteen

'Are you expecting anyone?' Alex snuck up on us again. He surprised me every time and I jumped involuntarily. I expect he did it on purpose. The slight upturn of his crooked lip came about as close to a smile as he could get.

'Why do you ask?'

'There's a lot of communication out there, some of it is centred around a group of paranormals making their way to this general vicinity. It would be logical to assume they are coming here.'

I looked to the rest of the team gathered in the meeting room. Ash, Metisse, Charmine, Mariah and me were all pouring over screens showing maps of where we suspected the Council's lockups to be.

More and more paranormals were disappearing. We deduced the Council was responsible and had hopefully not killed them but incarcerated them somewhere to use as blackmail.

This search was about more than just my mother. The Council reigned by terror. They snatched people from their beds in the middel of the night, took them from their families and used them as leverage to keep whole communities in line. It would make sense to keep them alive. We intended to liberate them.

'Do we know of anyone coming?' I asked.

Sometimes refugees just showed up, but most of the time we knew in advance. We had to. We couldn't just believe everyone was an ally. People had to be screened for their—and our—safety.

Gabriel and Ash shook their heads. Nope. They weren't expecting anyone. Metisse, Mariah and Charmaine glanced at each other in a suspicious way. I cocked my head. 'Charmaine?'

She sighed and nodded. 'We wanted it to be a surprise. Something nice in all of this stress. To cheer you up.'

'What surprise?' I was intrigued now.

Again they glanced at each other, only now both mother and son had a big smile on their faces.

'Your family,' Charmaine finally answered.

My brow creased in confusion. What family?

'Your mother's clan,' Metisse chimed in.

'My mother's clan?' I felt tingles all over my body. Could it be? I'd never entertained the idea of family before. No further than my mother and father. Stupid really. I mean, my mother did have a clan. She must have had a family, maybe siblings, parents. Who knows, maybe even other children. From before she met my father. That's the thing with immortals. We live so long many of us have multiple families over our endless lifespan.

Why hadn't I thought of that before. I could have searched for them, but I was so busy trying to avenge her death the thought never even crossed my mind.

Come to think of it, my mother never mentioned her

family, or her clan. Why not? Surely she must have missed them. A feeling of unease slowly pushed the warmth away as more and more questions filled my head.

'Your cousin,' Charmaine added softly as she took my hands. She had noticed my inner turmoil. 'She's the daughter of Embre's brother.'

'Why didn't she tell me?' I asked. 'Why didn't she say we had family? We could have gone there, been safe.' It didn't make sense. All those years on the run hiding from the Council, when we could have just gone to our kin. They would have protected us. They would have given us a home.

Charmane closed her eyes. When she opened them again there were tears at the edges. I watched one drop as it left her eye and slowly made its way down her cheek to the edge of her chin.

She took a deep breath and squeezed my hands. 'Your mother's clan banished her when she married your father.'

I felt my face flare up from the intense anger that spread from my very core up through my neck to my head. 'Banished her?' I repeated barely audible. 'They ostracised her because of her choice?'

Charmaine nodded. I tried to pull my hands away, disgusted at the actions of the Sabres. It wasn't fair, Charmaine hadn't done that, she was my mother;'s friend, but I projected it on all Sabres. I wasn't thinking straight.

She held on and continued the connection. 'They were scared. They didn't know what they were doing,'

'They should have.' My voice gained in strength again. I looked around. Metisse avoided my gaze. Gabriel's normally soft grey eyes were bright red, his anger mirroring mine.

'Yes,' Charmaine agreed. 'They should have been more

open-minded. More forgiving.' She squeezed my hands again and I turned my gaze back to her. 'They are now. Give them a chance, Trish. Please. Be better. Do not repeat the mistake.'

'Forgiving?' My vision was tinted red and fur sprouted all over my back. I didn't have to look to know it was a combination of black and ochre. I didn't even try to stop it from happening. 'Forgiving for what? For loving each other?' You all make it sound as though they were criminals. As though they did something unspeakable. They loved each other. They looked further than all of your petty discrimination to the souls inside and they were punished for that? For me?'

'The clan did not know, Trish. They were narrow-minded. Afraid of what they didn't understand.' Ash came over to us. 'They prospect of a romance between Wolves and Sabres was unheard of. They had to battle against the separatism prevalent then.'

I turned my anger to him.

'And now.' I looked purposely towards Mariah and Metisse. They both still held the superiority ideas that caused them to look down on the Wolves. I turned back to my big friend.

'That doesn't give them the right to send us away,' I shouted. 'They could have helped. They could have protected us.'

I pulled myself free from Charmain's hands and stepped back before I lashed out in anger.

Tears of anger and pain spilled down my face.

'They could have saved her,' I whispered.

As I stormed out of the room, I saw Gabriel come after me, but Ash stopped him with a hand on his arm.

The big man was right. I didn't want to see anyone now.

Not even Gabe, I had to be alone. I had to process this. This rejection.

I sat on the ledge overlooking the stream and threw yet another stone into the flowing water. It splashed loudly and broke the peace. The ripples were big at the contact point but quickly flowed outwards and lost their strength, depleting in the calm as the natural flow took over the movement.

My anger receded much in the same way and was replaced by sadness that gripped me with a vengeance. I felt alone. Completely lonely. And so very, very guilty.

Once again I was gaining insight in what my mother, and possibly my father too, had given up because of me. They both probably even died because of me. Now I knew my mother was banished because of me. The pain in my heart threatened to engulf me and my breathing came in gasps. Tears flowed down my face onto my clenched fists.

'Breathe,' a voice inside me shouted. Breathe, live, otherwise it has all been for nothing. If I died now, if I gave up, my parents would have suffered in vain. I had a duty to go on.

Breathe.

In.

Out.

I took deep gulps of air through my nose and forced myself to take it deep into my torso. My lungs filled. I held my breath and pushed the panic down. Then I let the air out through my mouth.

Breathe.

Repeat.

Slowly I forced the grief to the background. It would have to wait. There was no time to mourn now. Not with the Council vamping up its attacks on the refugees searching us out.

My eyes were closed as I compelled my body to relax. I focussed on the cool air around me as it blew past my face. On the sound of the water in the stream. I breathed in sync with the rippling water. Slowly, as the stream flowed over the rocks in the centre of the small waterway, I felt the tightness of my muscles seep out of my body into the stone of the ledge beneath me.

Small variations of the airflow alerted me to the presence of someone else. The scent was familiar and filled me with warmth.

It was Ash. My rock. Even more than my two beaus, if I was really honest, there was all of the love without the complications.

I felt him sit down on the ledge next to me. The warmth of his body called to me and I leant into him as he put his massive arm around my shoulders.

Words weren't necessary and we sat that way for what must have been at least fifteen minutes. I let the cleansing heat of the Shaman seep into my body and push the loneliness to the background. I would never be alone, as long as I had my mentor.

'You okay?' Ash asked. He knew the answer, he felt the calm in my frame. I nodded. He lightly kissed my head. Like a father. A protector.

Ash was my family. Like Metisse and Gabriel. And Charmaine. I did have family. Maybe not by blood, but never the less definitely family.

'Why do they hate each other so much, Ash?' I asked

after another comfortable silence. There was no anger in my voice, just a need to know.

'I don't know,' he answered to my disappointment. 'It has always been this way between Wolves and Sabres. Even before we passed over the land bridge. It could be something deep in nature. You see predators arguing over hunting territories. Maybe that's the basis.'

It sounded logical, but there had to be more. 'But we're not governed by pure instincts anymore, are we?'

'Yes and no. I mean, if you look; interactions between humans and paranormals alike, they still fight each other and amongst themselves for power over land, countries and sometimes the world. We are not so far from our origins as we would like to be.'

'No, I guess not.'

'And then there's the cat and dog thing.' I felt him smile. He was of course, of neither persuasion. The neutral onlooker if you will. I guess it must seem very silly to him sometimes.

'But we don't have to. Not anymore,' I tried again. 'Cats and dogs can get along. If they are taught from cub to live together, they do. No problems. If they learn to love instead of hate.'

'Very true, Trish. But old understandings run deep. We immortals have long memories. It is hard to forget previous indiscretions.'

I guess that was true. Immortality was not always a blessing. Long lives meant there were old ideas and old hatred that festered and were difficult to dislodge.

'It's up to you to change their minds,' Ash suggested.

'Great,' I complained. 'No pressure.' He kissed the top of my head again and laughed.

'Nope, none.'
I smiled.
It could be done.
And I do love a challenge.

Chapter Nineteen

Back at the compound the team discussed how to handle the intended ambush.

We had to act fast, my emotional breakdown cost us enough time as it was. There was no more to lose.

The clan members were on their way and, if nothing happened, would arrive before noon tomorrow. They were travelling in two SUVs taking the back routes, even some off-road trails to make sure they weren't seen by the Council.

But the Council knew about their plans.

'They know the gist of the route,' Alex informed us. We left the "how" for the moment. We needed to act.

'Does your information say anything about where they will attack the cars?' Gabriel asked.

'Not specifically, but it does mention it is distanced enough from Weisland to avoid any "interference" from us.'

'Okay.' Gabriel leant over the screen showing the region on the app that resembled Google Maps but offered more deviance of the normal routes.

A red wriggly line and two flags showed the intended route from Canada to our compound. It was very circuitous. They kept to the forest and back roads avoiding any towns or highways. Even the border crossing was clandestine.

I was surprised at the level of detail Mariah and Charmaine supplied. They had been working on this for a while.

Gabe placed his fingers on the screen and pulled to the side, enlarging the detail of the map. He started from Weisland and went steadily further up the intended route.

'We're looking for an ambush site. Something we would use if we were the agressor,' he explained.

Metisse and Mariah joined him in the scrutiny of the terrain. I watched from the side, my mind going over the possibilities of each area Gabriel magnified. My assassin skills and instincts were now an asset.

We searched for canyons, rivers they might have to cross, black-out spots in the grid and phone reception. Anything that would offer an edge for the attackers.

They had to stop the cars, one way or the other. A narrow road would be an option. Some place where reversing would not be possible. That was what I would do.

'Do we know where they are now?' I asked. Charmaine shook her head. The creases in her brow displayed the anxiety for her friends.

'Can't we contact them?' Metisse asked, voicing my thoughts exactly.

'No,' Mariah answered. 'We agreed there would be total silence so the Council couldn't track them.'

'Yeah, but neither can we.'

'True.' She shrugged.'

Can't we send a message, or anything.?'

'They turned off their phones. To be sure.'

'So we're all in the dark.' I stated.

'That about covers it. Yes.' Mariah sent dark looks my way, as usual. We still didn't get on. I hadn't meant it as a reproach, but she had definitely understood it that way. Whatever.

We slaved over the images for more than two hours until we settled on two possible locations. One, a bit closer to Weisland, on a cliff road. Narrow and steep. The cars would have to slow down to navigate the hazardous terrain. The high vegetation offered hiding places for any attackers.

The second option was at a river crossing on an off-road trail where they would cross the border illicitly. The river wasn't very wide, but the satellite picture showed many rocks and fast flowing white topped currents. The cars would have to cross one by one, slowly and carefully. Like in the first option, the banks offered a lot of cover for any would-be attackers.

We decided to cover both options. We would split up into two groups and each take one to the possible ambush sites.

We had an advantage because the Council didn't know we were aware of their plans. At least we hoped they didn't. The investigation of the past days when we searched for a mole came to mind. I hoped that we had been right. That there wasn't one.

'We'll keep the details to just this team,' Charmaine said. 'Gather the squads and only tell them we have a mission. No more. The fewer who know where we're going, the better our chances to pull this off.'

Nods all around. No one wanted to voice the possibility of a traitor. We would tackle that later, when we got back.

We proceeded to spilt the team in two. Metisse would lead one, Gabriel the other. We agreed both teams had to be a combination of Wolves and Sabres. It was a political statement but also just common sense. They had to learn to work together and also it would send a good message to the visiting Clan. Mariah argued only Sabres should go, as they would be more familiar to the guests.

'That is exactly why the teams should be a combination of both,' I intervened. 'They can get used to the fact this is a cooperation right from the start. We work together here. All persuasions.' She turned her dark looks on me again. 'No exceptions,' I added to make my point.

'Trish is right, Mariah,' Charmaine supported me. 'They know the rebellion is a collaboration of all paranormals. We need to show this in all our actions. Not just to Sabres, to all paranormals. This is a new time. New rules.'

'I will join Gabriel's team,' Ash suggested.

'Okay,' I answered. 'Then I'll go with Metisse.'

That shocked them all. I saw lots of wide open eyes.

'Hell no,' Metisse said. I cocked my head at him in question.

Unexpectedly, Gabriel came to his rescue. 'He's right, Trish. Though, maybe not in his wording.' He had to do that, stab at his love rival, couldn't stop himself from a bit of criticism. 'You are much to valuable to the cause. We can't risk you getting hurt in a battle.'

Lots of nods. Even from the big man. Though he was a bit more reserved than the rest.

'What?' I answered with a hollow laugh. 'You serious?'

Metisse hesitated. He obviously recognised I was vexed. 'Yes,' he finally said.

I looked around at the team. I knew they were worried about me, but this was not going to happen. I decided to try a more political approach than my usual jump-at-their-throat manner.

'These people are all here because of me,' I started.

'They came here because I'm supposed to be the Lamaq. The one who frees them from the oppression of the Council.'

I saw a smile begin to grow on Ash's face.

'They look to me to lead them in this war against the Council.' I continued. 'How would it look if I remained here, safe in the compound, while I sent others to the first fight with our enemy?'

That silenced them.

'I can't ask people to die for me and be absent myself. If I'm to be this chosen one, I have to be there. I have to help with more than just my image. I have to be hands-on, show our people we all need to do this together.' I saw shy nods. I was getting good at this politics thing.

'I have to go. I have to be on the frontline. I have to lead.' I stopped at that. It occurred to me to point out that this was what I did. I was an assassin, I knew ambushes. I knew killing. But when I glanced at Ash he winked and very slightly shook his head, so I decided to take his unspoken advice and just leave it at that.

'You're right, Trish,' Charmaine acknowledged. 'You have to be seen championing the cause.'

Thanks Charmaine, I said to myself. I would thank her out-loud later.

Gabriel looked unconvinced.

'If you insist on going,' he started. So I nodded that I did. 'Then you should be with my team. We can protect you.'

'You think we can't?' As expected Metisse took the bait. 'Trish will be safer with us.'

'Ash and I can protect her in ways you can't,' Gabriel countered.

'Like how?'

Oh shit.

Here we go again.

They continued to insult each other's prowess in keeping me safe. I closed my eyes and willed them to shut up.

Nope. It didn't happen. They were still at it.

'Stop it, guys,' I shouted above their heated voices.

Both looked at me with a hurt look on their faces. Gabriel was about to say something when I raised one eyebrow. He knew me well enough to shut up. Metisse on the other hand, failed to notice and had to have the last word.

'He can't protect you like…' in the ensuing heavy silence it finally dawned on him this was not the place, or the time, to push his point. After all, I had said I would be joining his team. Like Gabriel, he closed his mouth with an audible snap and looked somewhat contrite.

'I will be joining in the mission,' I stated very adamantly. 'I will take care I don't put myself in needless danger. I am a trained assassin, in case you forgot. I know how to protect myself.' I emphasised the last point. No one needed to protect me. I was perfectly able to do that myself, thank you. 'Let's get this done.'

After that we got down to the details. Who would we approach to join us in the mission. We needed two teams of six to eight people. A mix of Wolves and Sabres. I insisted we have Stephan and one or two of his people in the teams. He had made it very clear he wanted some action, now he would get it. But only if he followed orders.

'I'll speak to him,' Gabriel offered.

Chapter Twenty

Gabriel's group took the cliff pass and we went to the river crossing.

There were six in our merry band. Two Wolves from Gabriel's pack, one from Stephan's, a Sabre, Metisse and me. The Wolves were all very gung-ho and Gabriel admonished them before we left. They would follow orders. Mine.

Metisse, of course, was not happy with their presence. But that was tough. He would have to live with it.

Gabriel insisted that Moses—his enforcer—join us. I guess he still didn't believe Metisse could keep me safe. Thanks for the confidence guys.

We piled into the four-wheel drives and started on our way to the border. Moses drove the first car with me and Metisse in it, the others followed. We sped over the highway to reach the general vicinity as quickly as possible. It was a risk, but so was coming too late. We had to get there in advance of our guests and hopefully find the Council's team before things went south.

The weather deteriorated the closer we got to the

border. Rain pelted the roof of the car and Moses had to slow down due to aquaplaning.

When we finally left the highway and made our way over small back roads on a hardly visible dirt-track, the rain was coming down in sheets. It would make the mission more of a challenge, but on the other hand, it would also hinder the Council's team.

'We're about two or three hundred metres from the river,' Moses announced three hours later, as he stopped the car under a large tree that gave us a semblance of cover from the onslaught.

We gathered our weapons and left the vehicle.

The Wolves and the Sabre changed, preferring to work with built-in weapons. Metisse and I stayed in human form. A combination of Wolves and Sabres without any explanation would be a risk with the Canadian clan. They might confuse us with a threat. In our plans we counted on the heightened senses we all had when in animal form, but the Wolves' noses were useless in all this rain. We would just have to wing it.

The big grey wolf I recognised as Moses took point. He led the way up the side of the hill. My feet slipped repeatedly in the mud and slick mulch on the forest floor. I regretted my earlier decision, claws on four feet were a definite benefit in these circumstances. I trudged onwards.

Slowly the rain abated. It looked like we were through the worst of it. The sun rose to the east and lightened up the dark forest we moved through. The deep black clouds diffused the strength of the sun and the light was hazy. Long shadows were cast over the forest floor and we used them as cover the closer we got to the river.

I could hear the sound of the water rushing over the rocks. The deluge would have swollen the river. That meant the clan's cars would have to go even slower than we initially calculated. It helped us in a way and gave us more time to get to the location.

Moses took us even higher up the hill. He wanted the vantage point in case the Council's assassins were already here.

We found a small ledge with a cave that offered some shelter and Metisse and I scanned the area. Moses took the Wolves to recon and the Sabre slunk off into the forest.

I placed the semi automatic on the floor of the ledge and checked the sword on my back. I prefer a sword any day. Guns run out of bullets, the cutting edge on a sword is there to stay. In the hands of an experienced assassin— which I am—a sword is the weapon of choice.

Metisse joined me and we searched the line of the river we could see from our vantage point.

'Nothing yet,' Metisse said as he sat down next to me. I smiled. I loved the way he always stated the obvious so seriously. It was endearing.

I smiled. It lit up his face. He's such a sweet guy some times. The absence of his love rival noticeably lowered the tension in Metisse. He was back to his normal self. I welcomed it.

'They will probably have some delay because of the rain,' I answered. Metisse nodded. He continued to scan the dirt road on the horizon while I watched the fauna on both sides of the shallow, but fast flowing river.

One of the Wolves came back. He changed back into human form to bring us up to speed on what they had found.

'This is the spot,' he started. 'We found tracks of at least six people, maybe more, the rain has washed everything else away. And the place stinks of gun oil. One of the others found two people hiding in the foliage, they're watching the river crossing.'

'Six, at least?' He nodded again.

'We know where three of the others are, the rest are still out of view. We stayed back so we could regroup and decide what to do.'

'Good call,' Metisse said. I saw the tactician in him surface. 'That they are still here means the convoy hasn't passed yet.' We all nodded. 'We need to take them out before they arrive.'

At that precise moment we heard the Wolf howl pierce the sounds of the forest.

I turned my attention to the horizon where the first of the two SUVs made its slow and careful decent over the ridge down to the river.

'Shit,' the Wolf said and changed in one fluid motion to run back into the forest in the direction of the river. Another howl answered the first and we knew our cover was compromised. I just hoped both of the Wolves were okay. The sound of the last howl was mixed with a yelp of pain.

Metisse and I grabbed our weapons and made a quick dash down the slippery hillside towards the quickly unfolding drama.

The second car crested the ridge and, with its predecessor now navigating the river, made its way down to follow.

It had moved another twenty metres when the assassins opened fire on both vehicles. Rapid gunfire from automatic weapons stitched holes on both cars. The inhabitants ducked at the first impact and the second car swerved sideways to protect the passengers from the onslaught.

I heard a cry and a snarl, and deduced there was now one assassin less. Another changed the direction of his gun to stop two oncoming Wolves. They swerved at the last possible moment and one barrelled right over him. The second Wolf grabbed the downed man by the throat and ripped it out viciously, effectively ending the threat from that side.

The assassins realised they were being attacked themselves and tried to regroup. One large man shouted orders and emptied his automatic in the direction of the Sabre charging him. The cat swerved mid--stride but was unable to avoid all the bullets. It thundered to the ground twitching and scratching at the slippery mud in an attempt to right itself.

'Bordon!' I shouted at the top of my voice and the man turned to me.

The sound of his name in the midst of the fight was definitely not what he expected.

It gave the cat just enough time to get to its feet. I motioned it to leave with a big sway of my arm as I ran onto the bank of the river. I heard Metisse crash through the foliage after me and continue to my right where more assassins concentrated on the SUV in the river.

'You!' the big assassin shouted over the sound of the river. A vicious smile adorned his hard face. He lowered the gun. I understood immediately. This would not be a gun fight. Not between him and me.

Bordon towered over me by at least twenty centimetres. He had more than fifty pounds on me. A massive man by all accounts. He was one of the Council's top assassins. The top-dog probably, now I'd gone over to the other side.

He hated my guts. No problem, the feeling was completely mutual. The man was a psychopath. He relished in long painful deaths. Skinning his victims was one of his calling cards. Not a nice man. Taking him out would be a pleasure.

'What a bonus,' his voice was cold, threatening and full of vicious promise. Good thing I'm not easily impressed.

'Ditto,' I answered.

'Let's do this the old way,' he continued. 'Shooting you would be too easy. I want you to scream. I will bring your skinned pelt back to the Council and claim my reward.'

I just stared at him.

'You betrayed the paranormal world,' he continued as we circled each other warily.

'That depends on your perspective,' I answered.

'You collude with rebels, lowly Werewolves and Sabres. You abused the trust the leaders had in you. You are a traitor.' He continued his ranting, it was getting tiresome and I yawned. As expected it incensed him even more. That was exactly what I wanted.

'Yada, yada, yada. You always did talk too much,' I taunted.

Bordon threw his machine gun to the ground and pulled a vicious looking sword from its scabbard on his back. It was big, black and very sharp. He twirled it around in circles to show off his prowess.

Big deal. He had brawn, buckets full of self-confidence and a lot of muscle. But that wouldn't help. It would come down to who the clever one was here. And believe me, that wasn't him.

From the corner of my eye I saw the fight continue around me. Most of the assassins had run out of bullets and were now in hand-to-hand combat with our guys and the Sabres who spilled from the cars. There were more than the original six assassin the Wolves had counted. Not a problem, our numbers had swelled too with the visitors. Now I could concentrate on my own fight; Bordon. The piece of shit in front of me.

He advanced a slow step, walking on the balls of his feet, while I unsheathed my own sword. I held eye contact. The eyes would tell me what he was going to do. He moved another short step.

Sure enough, he blinked just before he rushed me. I was prepared and ducked to the side as his sword swished over my head. I struck out with my blade and made contact with the thick leather armour he wore. I drew blood, but not as much as I wanted. The leather had done its job. Bummer.

Bordon recovered quickly, affirming my suspicion the guy had no feelings at all. Nothing registered. Not even his own pain.

He turned quickly and slashed. I ducked and moved backwards. We circled each other and he attacked again. Our swords connected and he pushed, hoping to unbalance me. He expected me to counter his push, I didn't. I surprise him by moving backwards. This caused him to lose his footing and he stumbled after me. I swiped the sword towards his exposed torso, but slipped on the wet rocks and almost went down.

The smile returned to his face as he pushed onwards and tried to force me into the water. I reversed and side-stepped at the same time, then rushed him with my sword point moving rapidly from side to side. The effect was like a screen and he didn't know where the cutting edge was until it hit him in the thigh. The blade drew serious blood that quickly coloured the water bright red.

Bordon screamed in anger. I don't think losing had ever crossed his mind. He was that arrogant. Just his size advantage was enough to convince him he would be the victor. Now I had drawn blood, not once, but twice. He was becoming extremely mad. Exactly what I wanted. Anger would cloud his vision and the few cohesive thoughts he had. It would give me the edge.

His face contorted in a grimace of outrage. The nostrils flared and he bared his teeth at me. Who was the animal now?

For a second I hoped I hadn't misjudged my advantage. But it was too late now anyway.

He rushed me again. I swerved and he careened past me. I slashed, but missed. This time he turned quickly and caught me off guard. He put all his strength into a his assault and the two swords clashed with a terrible shock. It knocked the heft out of my hand and my sword clattered to the ground, but not before it shattered his blade.

We both recoiled from the massive impact. Bordon was on one knee. His gaze went from the remnants of his blade to mine that lay more than three metres from me and two from him. That gave him the upper-hand. We both knew it was out of reach for me now. I had to think fast.

He stood up and, instead of going for the sword, advanced on me, cracking his knuckles. I could see the relish this situation was giving him. His arrogance once again clouded any common sense he might have possessed.

He outweighed and out-sized me. In a normal world I wouldn't have stood a chance.

But this wasn't a normal world. And I definitely wasn't a normal woman.

I let the Sabre's claws drop into my hands and waited for him to come to me.

It didn't take long. He was elated with the perceived advantage. It made him complacent and he didn't notice the built-in weapons that sprouted from my fingers. Ten centimetre claws adorned both of my hands. And more than that, I knew how to use them.

Bordon reached to his back and pulled a wicked looking combat knife from a hidden scabbard. He passed it from hand to hand in yet another attempt to impress me or scare me. He achieved neither. I continued to watch his eyes. He had a habit of squinting just before he attacked. That was all I needed to follow. Not the ridiculous knife, nor his fancy footwork. I stood my ground and waited.

Sure enough, his eyes narrowed and less than a second later he rushed me, slashing the knife wildly at my throat hight. It might have worked if I hadn't taken a step forward too and dropped to my knees. I slid over the mud under his reach and brought my claws up to slash his side at the point where the leather armour ended around his waist. The resulting impact and spray of blood was encouraging.

I slid further and turned to face him again. He skidded over the mud and came to a stop on his knees five metres from me. His left hand was pressed to the wound in his side, deep red blood gushed between his fingers and coloured the mud. He pressed himself up from the ground with his right hand and turned to face me.

If looks could kill, I would have been incinerated. I think he'd never entertained the idea that I might actually be able to hurt him. Well, bummer. I planned to make his bad day even worse.

He tried to stand up straight. The sweat dripped off his face and the tightness of his brow defied the image he wanted to portray. He definitely wasn't okay. Not even close.

He advanced on me again. Slower this time. The knife was still in his right hand. He hadn't let go.

Pity. Now I'd have to take it from him. His gaze was fixed on my hands, or more pertinent, on the massive claws that were now stained with his blood. I held my hands up to show him the weapons I had. The smile on my face and the contempt I didn't even try to conceal pushed him to attack again.

Not a good idea.

He rushed me. I ducked to the right—his left—at the last moment, turned and slashed my claws over the back of his hamstrings as he careered past me. He went down like a brick wall.

I took the opportunity to look around a bit. The fight was coming to an end. Two Sabres I didn't know made short work of an assassin. The Wolves had joined forces with another Sabre and taken on two black-clad enemies who no longer resembled human beings. It was a massacre. The combined forces of our team with the occupants of the SUV's annihilated the ambushers.

I decided to stop playing around and walked up to Bordon. He was hunched over on his knees with one hand in the mud. The rain and mud was bright red around him. The wound in his side and the ones on the back of his thigh pumped out bright red artery blood. He was bleeding out.

I could have just left him there. Let nature do its job. But I decided to finish it. Not that I was getting squeamish or wanted to save him any agony. No, I had to be sure that he died. The only way was to kill him now. I straddled his back and pulled his head back.

'See you in hell,' I said as my claws dug deep into his throat. I pulled my arm back and to the side taking most of his neck with me. I let go of the corpse and made my way to the congregated good-guys standing next to the SUV on the bank of the river.

'Anyone hurt?' I asked.

'No one seriously,' Metisse answered.

'Do the cars still work?'

Metisse nodded. Good. Tough cars.

I wanted to get out of here as quickly as possible. There was no guarantee the Council hadn't sent a back up team. I would have. The sooner we left, the safer we would be.

I turned and made my way to the back of the SUV and jumped in without a word. The visitors would take us to our own vehicles, from there we would lead them out of the forest and back to base. Secrecy wasn't needed anymore so we made good time and were on the hard top before the hour had passed.

Moses contacted Gabriel's team and informed them we had the visitors.

When we rolled into the Sabre compound we saw Gabriel's team had beaten us to it. They stood next to their two four-wheelers. Ash was attending to one of the Wolves. Seems like we weren't the only ones to see combat today.

Gabriel opened my door before I could and reached in to help me disembark. He looked me over and smiled. 'Yes, I'm allright.' I reassured him.

'And that?' He pointed to the blood on the back of my shirt.

'Not mine.'

He kissed me tenderly and held me close.

'Good,' he answered softly. I realised how concerned he had been. I smiled up at him. The love in his soft grey eyes warmed me.

'What did you expect?' Metisse's venomous voice broke the moment. 'I told you I would take care of her.' He challenged Gabriel who's hold on me became more possessive.

I closed my eyes and exhaled loudly. 'And I told you both I can take care of myself.'

I turned to face both of them. Their posture screamed aggression, both of them.

'Really guys?' I was exasperated. 'Now?'

I stomped off. Fuck this.

I walked over to the visitors and Charmaine.

'Lets have everyone checked out and then get some sleep. We can talk tomorrow, when we're all a bit more rested.'

'Good idea, Trish,' Charmaine agreed.

I smiled at her, kissed her on the cheek and turned to the cars. I was happy I could at least cool down before I really met my relatives properly. I still had mixed feelings about them and how they had treated my mother. I needed some time to calm doen before I tackled that.

Metisse followed me to the cars.

'Aren't you staying?' he asked. His face was on the verge of panic.

'No way,' I answered, still mad. 'Not with you acting like a teenager.' From the corner of my eye I saw Gabriel looking smug.'

'What about Gabriel? He's no better.' Metisse just proved my point. Stupid.

'No, he isn't,' I said to both their surprise. 'And that is why I'm sleeping alone tonight. Both of you; grow up, will you?'

With that, I stomped off. 'Moses, can I beg a lift from you?' I called out to the pack enforcer. He looked sheepishly at me, then at his alpha and back to me. He nodded.

'Yeah, sure Trish.'

I pulled open the passenger door and sat down, impatiently waiting for him to leave. Moses thankfully decided not to wait for anyone else and joined me. We set out for the Wolf compound in silence.

I slept alone that night. It was quiet. Nice really. I was so sick of the constant bickering between the two of them.

I usually alternated between my lovers; one night Gabriel stayed over, the next Metisse, and so on. It was a good arrangement from my perspective. Simple and fair.

Initially, they agreed.

So, why did they have to argue every night? Inevitably one of them would be sulking when I said good night. The other would have a triumphant look on his smug face. Again, Metisse was the worst, but Gabriel was gaining. I was sick of it.

Instead of feeling good with whichever one of them I was with, I ended up feeling guilty about leaving the other alone. It ate me up inside. Add the constant tension in the air whenever all three of us were in the same room, and you get an idea of how I felt.

Single felt like such a good idea right now.

Next morning the Sabres joined us in the Wolves' compound. Charmaine and a slightly nervous Metisse brought the visitors.

Charmaine came over to me, followers by a tall man and a stringy woman. Both had stern faces and measured movements.

My friend look my hands and greeted me warmly. Charmaine always did. She was like that. Not to make a point, even. Though it definitely did, no this was just her.

She turned her head towards the man standing next to her wheelchair.

'Trish,' she said softly. 'This is Vincent. The chieftain of the Ottawa Clan. And his sister Bailey, the enforcer. They are your cousins.'

Right. Dilema.

What do you do when faced with unknown relatives? Do you shake hands, just nod your head or break out in sobs and fall in each other's arms? The last was a definite no. I was still mad at the betrayal.

I settled on a nod. Kind of cowardly, in hindsight.

I saw Vincent struggled with the same uncertainty. Bailey was easier, she was much more sure in her return nod. God, this was uncomfortable.

'This is awkward,' Vincent stated. His voice was deep, dark. There was a soft undertone in the words he said. He tried to laugh it off a bit, but wasn't very successful.

'It is,' I agreed.

I looked at Charmaine who squeezed my left hand in support.

'Welcome to our compound.' I tried to sound sincere.

I really did want to welcome them. It was just that nagging voice at the back of my mind that they were the reason my mother wasn't here. I know, it wasn't fair. But neither was them ostracising her. And me.

'Thank you,' the man continued. 'My father and your mother are siblings.' His face coloured as he realised what he had said. 'They were siblings.' He corrected himself but the harm was already done. He didn't know there was a chance that she was still alive, and I wasn't about to tell him. Not yet.

We'd see, depending on how things progressed.

It wasn't looking hopeful from where I was standing.

Vincent continued on a different subject. 'Thank you for intervening yesterday. The outcome would have been very different if your team had not been there.'

I nodded. They would have been overwhelmed. And they knew it.

'You're welcome,' I answered. 'It also gave us a good chance to decimate the Council's assassin force.'

We killed more than ten assassins in the two missions. Gabriel's team found another group at the second site. A fallback, in case the river ambush was unsuccessful.

The silence was heavy. I took a deep breath, about to say something, but I had no idea what to talk about. We were all very politely circumventing the elephant in the room. I glanced at Charmaine. She just smiled back. Great. Now what?

The silence weighed heavily on my shoulders. It felt like time stood still. I had no idea what to do now.

'I don't want to sound rude,' I said exasperated. 'But why are you here?'

It sounded blunt, crude, unfriendly. I didn't intend it to come out the way it did. I saw the pain it inflicted in Vincent's sharp intake of breath, his wide open eyes. Yeah, well welcome to my world; truth hurts.

I glanced at Charmaine again. Thankfully, she didn't look as shocked as the rest of the Sabres. She knows me better than most.

I looked around in the ensuing silence after my words. Ash stood next to the table, his arms over each other. Not in a tense manner, no; relaxed, quite the contrast to my own feelings. Gabriel stood next to him, slightly less at ease, but still calmer then me. Metisse was—as expected—shocked by my bad manners. Well, tough.

I think Vincent felt as awkward as I did. He looked at his sister then took a deep breath.

'We're here to offer our clan's help in the war against the Council.'

I looked at him intently. My eyes locked with his.

The brown of his irises had tints of ochre in them, a sure indication of his state of mind. The cat was coming through. I guess it felt a bit threatened, by the proximity of the Wolves and most likely, by me.

'You understand this is a joint venture?' I wanted to get any preconceived superiority out of the way immediately. 'We have many different paranormal creatures here. All are equal in this compound.' I almost said; "even the Wolves" but that was unnecessary. He understood.

'We'll gladly fight alongside any paranormal to free us all from the Council.'

'Are you sure about that?'

'Yes,' he answered without hesitation.

Vincent looked stronger than a minute ago. 'We will fight with anyone, anytime.' He made a point of looking at each person here in the room to emphasise his point. Then he looked back to me. His eyes were still warm. His features relaxed a bit as he took another step closer to me.

He took a deep breath.

'I'm sorry for the way our clan treated your mother,' he said to my surprise. 'And you. You didn't deserve that. Sure, there were other circumstances then and people were much more narrow-minded. But that doesn't change the fact you are family. The clan should never have sent you away.'

Okay, he was direct. I was glad for that. He took the bull

by the horns. Even if that didn't mean I would let him off easily.

'So what's changed?' I couldn't keep the anger out of my voice.

'Life changed.' I hadn't expected that. I cocked my head in question.

'We have new enemies. Ones that outshine any traditional opponents by miles. We should have known. Your mother warned us about the Council. She predicted what would happen; that they would crush us, take away our strength, kill our spirit. My father scoffed at her words. We were strong then, nothing could touch us. We ruled the forests and the cities, we were the alpha predators.'

That was where the arogance came from.

'Little by little, life has been sucked out of the clans until there is just a shadow left of what we used to be. Initially, my father and the elders blamed your mother.'

My anger flared again.

'They accused your parents of unleashing the Council's wrath because of their "unnatural" love. The Council preached purity of race. Mixed couples were frowned on. More than that, they were hunted and killed. Cantix even urged my father to kill his own sister—your mother—to stop the abomination as he put it.'

This had to sink in. It was much worse than I had ever imagined.

The animosity my parents faced for their love—for me —was astounding.

'This was not about you Trish, not at that time.' He correctly gauged my feelings. 'You weren't born yet, this was when your parents professed their love and tried to alleviate the traditional animosity between Sabres and Wolves.'

I looked up. Tears pushed at the edges of my eyes. I swallow hard.

'What changed?' I repeated.

'The woll finally dropped from our eyes. We saw what the Council was doing. They divide and conquer. They set fractions—species—against each other so attention is diverted from the Council's wrongdoings. They fill our hearts with hate,' the enforcer added.

'Your parents knew. They tried to tell us. But we were arrogant. We were stubborn in our hatred. We were blind.' Vincent continued.

'When my father refused to give up his sister he was tortured to within an inch of his life. As a punishment, our children were taken as hostages to live within the Council's castles, never to be seen again. We don't know what has become of them. They will be grown up now, if they are still alive. Our way of life was taken from us. We were pushed out of our houses, our businesses broken. We became the pariah we so arrogantly rejected in our previous life.'

'The clan members turned against my father, against each other in the clan. We were decimated. The once proud clan was no more. The Council had done its job well. Resentment prevailed.'

'Then, in the course of the next decades we opened our eyes to what was happening around us with other para-normal groups. One by one, the strong were broken. The Council was never the agressor, never overtly. But they were the cause. They instigated arguments and set brother against brother. Child against their parents. We saw what they did and we felt ashamed.' He took a deep breath.

'Ashamed we had been so blinded by perceived superiority, wealth and power, we hadn't listened to your parents. That we had done the Council's bidding unknowingly.'

The tension in my neck abated slightly. I wasn't completely pacified, but Vincent's words did get through to me. I realised I projected my loss and pain onto these people. They were not their parents. They had not been the ones in power at the time my parents came together. They were not to blame.

'We should have listened and joined your parents in their struggle against the Council. Instead we turned them away. Our elders paid the price for their arrogance and narrow-mindedness. We all lost loved ones. Some of the remaining are broken in spirit and body.'

I looked into his eyes. There was sorrow there, but also a fire.

'We will not make the same mistake twice,' Bailey picked up the narrative. 'We are here to join your crusade. We will fight along side you, with you, to free ALL paranormal creatures from the tyranny of the Council. You lead. We follow.'

The last sentence made their conviction abundantly clear. Sabres lead. Following others was not their style. I noticed that on a daily basis with Mariah and the Clan. It cost them.

My anger mellowed. It wasn't completely gone. The stubbornness I am regrettably known for refused to let go, but my animosity abated towards these people, who were after all my kin.

Family. A notion so foreign to me, I didn't know what to do.

I stuck out my hand and was rewarded with a big smile on Vincent's sad face. He took my hand in both of his. I returned the smile and then, I don't know why, pulled him into a hug.

A collective sigh around me informed me how everyone had been holding their breath. Vincent enveloped me in a massive bear hug, then let go and turned to Bailey. The smile on her otherwise stern and hard face softened her visage and I saw the warmth she was also capable of.

We hugged as well.

I realised my hesitation had been partly anger, and partly fear they would still reject me. I felt the muscles in my neck and back relax from a tension I didn't know I had. An ache at the base of my skull dulled to the background. My breaths deepened and the fresh air flowed unobstructed to every last cell of my lungs. Pinpricks at the back of my eyes heralded tears I really didn't want to shed.

'Let's get something to drink,' I tried to change the subject and in the meantime regain control over my raging emotions.

Again smiles. Vincent squeezed my shoulder in support. I guess my struggle was not as inconspicuous as I thought.

So this was what it felt like to have family.

Chapter Twenty-One

Sex with Gabriel was my release of choice today.

I wanted it hard and rough. I needed Gabriel to take me, hold me down, ravish my body. I pushed his buttons. Dug my nails into his back, even drew drops of blood. I pulled him to me, pushed my body up hard to meet his trusts. I wanted to lose myself over the edge of pleasure and pain.

My voice took on a hard tone. Unfriendly. Violent. The words were guttural. Dirty. My vision turned red. I wanted to go over the boundaries and move into the dark places.

Gabriel stopped. He pulled himself back and disentangled himself from my embrace.

'What are you doing?' I shouted.

The sudden distance felt like an ice cold shower. All heat drained out of my body and left me empty and angry.

He looked at me with pain in his eyes. 'This isn't love. Trish,' he answered in a soft voice. 'It's violence.'

His actions felt like I'd hit a brickwall, I didn't listen to his words. I didn't see the pain and love. I felt he rebuffed me.

'Never heard you complain before,' I spat out, daring him to take the bait. The anger was still there and it threatened to engulf me. I struck out. A fight was almost as good as hard sex. It would relieve the tension, the pressure and the anger.

Gabriel stayed composed. He refused to be baited. 'What's going on, Trish?'

'What the fuck do you think is going on,' I lashed out. All the pressure overflowed. 'I'm mad as hell about all the crap you put me through. You and Metisse. I need to get rid of the tension and you won't even help me.'

'I want to help you. But not like this. I feel used.'

My patience was non-existent. I had no use for his kindness now. I needed pain, hurt, to make me feel alive. 'Oh for God's sake,' I shouted. 'I only want to fuck. What good are you to me if you can't even do that?'

Gabriel recoiled. The look on his face registered through my anger. The intense pain my words caused was clear in his soft grey eyes. I instantly regretted my words and reached out to him. But it was too late. I couldn't retract what I had said.

'Gabriel, please,' I tried. 'I'm sorry. I didn't mean it.'

He pushed his body further from me and stood up from the bed. There were tears at the edge of his eyes.

I had truly hurt my lover. I had cut him to the bone. I felt so terrible. I sat up, my legs underneath my body and reached out to him again. Gabriel avoided my outstretched hand and stood up. He turned to pick up his clothes and started to dress.

'Gabe, please,' I tried again. My own tears pushed at the edge of my vision. A heavy weight sat in my gut.

'Too late for that,' he replied. His voice now colder. 'You need to think about what you want, Trish.'

'I know what I want.' I shouted. The anger was back. He was rejecting me, again. How could he do that? Now, when I needed him. When I felt so alone.

All the tension between my two beaus in the last weeks surfaced and pushed to the front of my mind. They were what, at that moment, seemed to be the biggest challenge I faced. They pushed me over the brink. Taunted me, instead of helping. They acted like children fighting over a toy, Well I wasn't a toy.

I struck again out in anger. 'I want to be able to concentrate on winning this stupid war. I don't have time for your stupid petty differences with Metisse. Stop being so bloody selfish and grow up. That will give me some peace.' I sat back on the bed, my back to the headboard, my arms crossed over my chest, and challenged him to answer me. He did, just not how I expected.

'Maybe that's the issue here, Trish,' he answered. 'Your perception. To you this sharing thing is petty. To us it isn't. It eats away at the very fabric of our lives. What we were brought up to believe. Our values. Our morals. Our dreams, even. You disrespect our feelings in this unnatural situation we are in. You pass it off as insignificant, trivial even, because it interferes with your plans.'

He walked to the door and turned a last time.

'Who's selfish now, Trish?'

Three hours later I still lay awake in bed and stared at the ceiling.

My anger hadn't abated. I was still mad as hell. I hadn't asked for all of this prophecy shit. No one consulted me on whether I wanted to be stuck with these expectations, the pressure. Even two soul-mates. I never asked for that. Didn't even want one, let alone two.

I wound myself up no end. Persuaded myself Gabe wasn't being fair. That he and Metisse were all ganging up on me.

They were.

…Weren't they?

I almost convinced myself.

Trouble was; whatever I told myself didn't change the fact that Gabriel was right.

Shit.

What the hell was I going to do now?

The next morning found me running through the forest in Wolf form. The long sleepless night cleared my thoughts. There had been nowhere to hide from the truth of Gabe's words.

I'd ranted. Thrown all kinds of things through the room and broken quite a few items in my rage. I'd cried out, shouted, wept, sat in utter silence. Nothing changed the emotions that surfaced unbidden.

Everything came back to one inevitable conclusion. Gabe was right. I was selfish. This whole prophecy and "chosen one" thing had gone straight to my head. Outwardly I disowned all the attention, but it corrupted me. Made me almost believe the whole world did rotate around me. That I was the most important person in the world.

My God, how had that happened? How had I become that person?

I felt ashamed.

This wasn't me.

I had to get my head straight and become the me I

should be again. The person I was, deep down inside. I needed fresh air.

Grounding.

In this difficult time I turned to what always gave me relief. I changed and ran. As a Wolf I felt the earth under my paws as I raced through the forest. The trees blurred as I sped up and pushed my body to its limits. My lungs filled with fresh freezing air, the cold shocked my system. But I continued to run.

On the horizon, the first rays of sun peaked over the hills and bathed the forest in light. I felt the warmth on my fur, it invigorated me and pushed me onwards.

I ran through the trees, over clearings, jumped streams, waded through wider rivers. With every mile I ran, I felt the tension seep out of my body. The stress of the past year bled out of my pores. My mind cleared. My body rejoiced.

I stopped at the top of a hill, threw back my head and howled. It felt so very good.

I turned and loped off again, fully one with nature. I found a peace I could never have established in human form. For this I needed the Wolf, or the Sabre. I needed the closeness to nature and the direct feel of it over my whole body. The wind, the earth, the water.

From the corner of my eye I saw the shadow of another Wolf running parallel to me at fifty metres. He matched my pace and together we continued to speed through the trees.

In a clearing the Wolf emerged into the sunlight and I recognised him as my soulmate Gabriel.

He'd followed me. Shadowed me to keep me safe. I felt an almost overwhelming warmth and love for him.

I slowed, the emotions threatening to engulf me. Gabe walked over to me and I pushed my face up against his. I licked his jowls and rubbed myself along his body. He reacted in kind and we were soon frolicking in the tall meadow grass. There was no tension anymore. Not between us, and not in me. We enjoyed the environment and each other.

Life was good again.

Later we lay in each other's arms, back in human form.

'I'm sorry Gabriel,' I started. He put his finger on my lips and smiled. He knew. I didn't have to say my apologies out loud.

'You're back,' he simply said. 'That's good enough for me.'

I kissed him.

We made love in the meadow.

Tenderly.

As it should be.

Chapter Twenty-Two

Back at the compound we changed to human form after our run and dressed in my house. I didn't need to sleep. I felt invigorated. Full of energy. Sleep would come later. We had breakfast and made our way to the communal building for the daily briefing.

'We have to find her.' I stated.

The leaders were all gathered in the communal house.

They knew who I was talking about; Embre, my mother.

'But not only her, we need to find and liberate all the Council's political prisoners.' I continued.

My new found clarity looked further than my personal needs. 'The Council has taken many of our kin hostage. They need to be freed before others can join us.' I looked at each of the group separately. Made eye contact and pressed my point home.

'There are too many who don't dare join the cause because their families are held by the Council. They are pressed into compliance. Not because they agree with the Council, but because if they speak out, their kin will die.'

We all knew people who had lost loved ones that way. The Council was brutal. They made examples of the "traitor's" kin to dissuade others from joining us. They were very, very effective.

'We're mounting an offensive to find where the Council keeps their prisoners and free them. We also need to make sure no new people can be taken. For that, anyone who shows any interest in our cause, needs to have a safe haven here. For them and their families. That will take a lot of organising. So I want to set up a task force to do the logistics.'

'We need everyone to pull their weight in all this. We can only do it if it's a team effort.'

'Gabriel, please liaise with our computer people on the possible locations they already identified.' Gabe nodded.

'Metisse, I need you to help me go through the information our team came up with yesterday. We have to sift the nonsense from the important subjects.' Metisse looked less than enthusiastic. 'I know, none of this is particularly exciting, but it has to be done.'

He reluctantly nodded.

I continued to pass out tasks and after five more minutes we parted ways, leaving me alone with my Sabre lover.

'Thanks, Metisse,' I smiled at him. He slowly defrosted and I guess finally understood it was just the two of us. I was rewarded with a big smile. There was an edge of mischief in his eyes.

I wondered how much work we would get done.

Chapter Twenty-Three

'Tell me about him, Ash. Please.'

'Ismael?'

I nodded. I needed to know more about my father. What kind of man was he?

I knew he was important in the Werewolf community, they'd told me all about that. He was one of the original three. One of the First. I found information about his achievements. How he forged a new life for a heavily perse-cuted species.

But I had no idea what kind of man he actually was. Was he a nice man? Loving? Or a hard man, scarred by his long years? I had to know. He was an integral part of me. Even if I never consciously met him while he was alive, I'm his daughter. Half of what I am, came from him. I wanted to get to know him, so I could get to know me.

Ash smiled. His face warmed as he looked at me. We were close. Very close. He knew what I was thinking most of the time. In the short time we'd known each other he proved to be the best friend I could ever have, a mentor and a confidant.

He never judged me. Let me make my own decisions, even if they weren't the right ones. He never pressed me or tried to influence me. Just answered my questions if he could.

'Your father was a warm and loving man. But also fierce and protective of those he loved.' Ash smiled at me and warmed my heart.

'I remember the first day I saw him,' he continued.

I held on to his every word. I needed to know more about my heritage, about the parents I'd barely known.

We settled down for a long story.

'He stepped off the long boat as the last of the three.'

The long boat. Ash was there, that first day that the Werewolves set foot on the new country. That was tens of centuries ago.

'The others were wary, their eyes and heads flitted from side to side as they watched the treeline for any sign of life.' Ash was a born story teller. 'Your father was more relaxed. He smiled as he looked at the new country. His smile went all the way up to his bright green eyes.'

'Green?'

'Yes,' he answered with another smile. 'Green, exactly like yours. You have your father's eyes.'

I knew green was a unique colour for a Werewolf's eyes. Generally most had dark brown hues that turned to deep red when angry or scared. I remembered how surprised I was when I noticed Gabriel's eye colour, a beautiful soft grey. I thought that was unique. I'd assumed my own colour came from my mother. Some cats have green eyes. Now I knew it was part of my father's gift. I felt the small pricks that heralded tears and tried to push them back. I missed the man I had never known. It cut me to my heart.

'I waited until they were more relaxed then made myself known. Again, the two others reacted warily, Ishmael beamed. His warm smile heralded the start of a deep friendship. A brotherhood. He laid his hand on his companion's arm and calmed them. Then he walked over to where I stood just outside the treeline on to the beach. He stopped about two feet from me and smiled.'

'It's a global language; smiling. So even with language issues we managed to make the first contact a good one. The three stayed at the village for more than a year, slowly learned our language as I learned their's, and became used to their new home.'

'Where did they come from?'

'Europe, or what that was in those days. We're talking about the early Middle Ages, somewhere in the twelve hundreds.'

'They came before the Conquistadors?'

'Yes. Long before. There have been many others who "found" this nation before it was officially discovered in European terms. Most of them assimilated into the native tribes, like The Three. Some moved onwards to other parts of either North- or South Amerika. The Three stayed where they landed.'

'Why did they come?' Images formed before my eyes of their life among the native tribes. All my fantasy revolved around the one green-eyed man with the loving smile. Slow tears started to find their way down my cheeks.

'The Wolves were heavily persecuted in Europe in the Middel Ages, and far beyond for that matter. The church hunted them down with a vengeance, labelling them the spawn of the devil. The hell hounds. The Three were the only remaining ones of their pack. Everyone else had been murdered. Women, children; no distinction was made. And all in the name of a God.'

The soft swirling of the colours in Ash's eyes became more erratic, the hues brighter and more pronounced than earlier; a clear sign he was angry. I felt the same. Everywhere we went, everywhere we encountered humans, we were viewed with suspicion, fear and often downright aggression. And they say we are the dangerous ones.

'They escaped from their homeland Ireland during a plague, on a small Norwegian boat where the captain needed extra hands and asked no questions. I suspect the crew just wanted to leave the plague-infested country behind as quickly as possible.'

'It was bound for Norway but never got there. The sailors were too late, they took ill and died one by one, leaving only the Wolves who were immune to the terrible virus the humans carried. Ishmael threw the bodies into the ocean and the three changed course. Norway would only offer a relatively short reprieve. The plague was rampant through out the whole continent and anyone who didn't contract it would stand out, especially three men together. They navigated by the stars, something Ishmael picked up from the captain, and eventually landed on the coast of what is now Newfoundland.'

I poured us both a glas of water from the pitcher on the table and pushed one towards Ash. He sipped the cool liquid before he continued his story.

'The other two stayed with the tribe while Ishmael and I took our leave and made our way steadily south towards where we are now. Here we joined the Blackfoot Tribe and lived happily for many, many years until the Europeans came. They brought their suspicions and hatred with them, along with greed and a total lack of respect for the land and everything on it.'

'Ismael had started another pack in the years with our native friends. He married several times and had children. They had children of their own, some with and some without the Werewolf gene.'

'I have siblings?' I asked surprised.

'Maybe,' he answered softly. His eyes once again pastel and loving. 'The children were half Wolf and half human. Not all children with the Werewolf gene are immortal. Only those where the gene is dominant. They have to be at least three quarters Wolf. As he was the only one here, that was impossible.'

I bit my upper lip. Again, family I had was lost. Then a thought struck me. 'What about me? I'm only half Wolf, but I've lived for a very long time and don't seem to age anymore.'

'You are half Wolf and half Sabre. Both are magical creatures. Both are basically immortal. So are you.'

I'd never really thought of myself as immortal. I guess I knew, I mean; I didn't age. But still it wasn't something I dwelled on. Especially as it was very relative. We "immortals" didn't live for ever. My own parents were examples. We could be killed. We were killed.

So much for eternal life.

'There could be others related to you,' Ash broke my reverie.' Occasionally Wolves came from Europe hidden among the settlers, though most of them didn't make it. And then of course there are the descendants of the other two who landed with your father that auspicious day.'

'Ishmael and I stayed with the tribe for most of the coming centuries, though we were forced to move every now and then to disperse any suspicions on the side of the settlers. Our longevity and seemingly good health were in dire contrast to the life expectancy of the original owners of this nation. The Blackfoot were moved around, as you know, from one barren land to another, until they were allowed to re-settle on what had been their ancient holy lands. That was when I returned to them. Ishmael continued to fight the settlers with other tribes. Early in the last century, he finally returned to us.'

There was pain the last sentence. I understood this was not because he came back, but what led him to come home. 'How was he?'

'Disillusioned.' Ash continued softly. I saw it pained him as much as me. 'The persecution his people endured in his native Europe was mirrored in the way the same people treated the tribes. Here again, the rightful owners lost all rights to what was their's. Despite all his dedication, another people he belonged to again lost everything. Ishmael became bitter. Hard. He built a wall around his heart. One even I could not penetrate.'

We were silent. What was there to say? The tears made their way over my face again, for my father's pain. For the suffering of the tribes.

'I thought I would never see my old friend again. Not the real one. But I was wrong.' Ash continued.

I looked up at his smiling face.

'Your mother; Embre.'

I nodded.

'She hacked away at the wall and resurrected the man he once was. She warmed his heart and soul in a way no

173

one ever had. Not in the centuries he'd roamed this planet. She was the part of him he missed. A liaison that should never have been, was the one that finally saved him.'

'How did they meet?'

He laughed. 'On opposite sides of an argument.'

Yes, I could imagine that.

'The Sabres had just settled in the area and the peace was fragile. More Sabres were called to protect the space the clan carved out for themselves; Sabres from other clans, one of these was your mother. In a skirmish at the border of their territory she came face to face with Ishmael. They fought. Neither won. I think they already felt there was more. Neither really tried. After that they looked each other up in secret and their love blossomed.'

Yep, that sounded like mum. Do everything opposite to what was expected. Question the rules. Push the boundaries. I definitely inherited that from her. And her recklessness. It must have been a right bomb when she chose the enemy.

'Bet that didn't go down well.' I laughed at the memory of my stubborn and strong-willed mother.

'No it didn't. With either of the fractions. The Sabres were disgusted. The Wolves astounded. But your parents were adamant. Their's was a true love. Deeper and more sincere than any I have ever witnessed.'

Then he added with a laugh, 'and both of them were so unbelievably stubborn and refused to abide by any rules they did not make themselves. They were so strong their respective tribes had to concede. Either that or lose the best leaders they ever had. You know the outcome of that.'

His face softened as he reached out and took my hand. 'And then you came.'

'Yeah,' I said bitterly. 'I came and fucked it all up again.'

174

'No.' He was firm. 'No, you enriched what they had. You made it perfect.'

Okay. We would agree to disagree on that one. I still blamed myself for their deaths, they were no longer here because of me.

Chapter Twenty-Four

'Is Cantix an Elemental? I asked Ash out of the blue one evening as we sat beside the fire.

Ash was next to me, Metisse and Gabriel were both sulking in their rooms. We'd had a row earlier and I wasn't in hurry to see either of them before they grew up.

Could take a while.

Ash looked up from the scroll he was reading. It was part of a collection one of the clans had brought. Ash insisted he look into anything that could offer even the smallest aid in our quest. I had no idea how he managed to house that vast amount of information into his one brain, but he did. He must be the best natural computer in the world.

'No,' he finally answered as he rolled up the scroll. Good. Story time.

'Though he does have some Elemental magic.' He added. Hmm, not good.

'He inherited that from his mother.'

Funny, I never pictured Cantix had a mother.

'The Elementals have been part of human society for so long they have taken over some of the characteristics.' Ash continued.

'We have the same emotions, anger and longing. We resemble humans in so many ways. But there was one thing we could not do. And that is reproduce. We are not able to have children. Most of our kind accepted that. We formed bonds with people who already had children, or we adopted. That sufficed for all but one.'

We settled down to a long tale.

'Faddon was an Elemental living with the native tribes of Canada. He travelled over the landbridge in the same group I did, but stayed up north while I moved steadily south. He was an introvert man. Not easily part of a community. Always on the edge. Even in that we have copied humans.'

'He observed the humans in his tribes. He saw the pleasure and love they received from their children and was acutely aware of the happiness he missed without a family of his own. That ate away at him. I suppose he had what is generally known as empty-nest syndrome. Only for him it lasted for hundreds of years.'

I felt for him. It must be very difficult. Especially for someone alone.

'He stole a child. A little girl. He wanted to raise her as his own, but had no idea how to do that. The child cried, it was hungry. Faddon couldn't produce milk, so he did the only thing he could; he used magic.'

Shivers jumped up my spine. Poor kid. Magic was no substitute for the love of a true parent. I at least spent the first twelve years of my life with my mother. She taught me to love.

'The child was nurtured with magic. It was saturated

with magic. It festered and turned her into an emotionless being. Faddon had no idea how to raise a human child. The only thing they had in common was magic. They experimented together. Often to the detriment of the animals in the forest, sometimes even the people. Their hermit life compounded their isolation. Faddon and his daughter distanced themselves from their charges as Elementals. They revelled in the perceived superiority over humans'.

'We Elementals tried to bring them back into the fold. We pleaded, threatened. anything. It backfired, and Faddon and his child grew even more distant. They included magical creatures in their experiments. Which made them look down on the paranormal society as well as the human one. They felt superior to everything.'

Then he dropped the first bomb

'That child was Aquanaris.' I was shocked, but if I'm honest, I guess it was what I expected him to say.

Man, she'd had a raw deal. It wasn't enough for me to forgive or even understand what she had done to me and my family, but I did pity her.

The second bomb was even more of a shock.

'Cantix inherited it from her.'

'What!' I exclaimed.

'He inherited the elemental magic from Aquanaris.'

'His mother?' I almost shouted incredulously.

Ash nodded.

'His mother?' I repeated, softer now. Again he nodded, but I had to say it out loud. 'Aquanaris is Cantix's mother?

'Yes.'

'Oh, my God.' I was truly stumped. Hadn't seen that one coming. Not in a million years.

'We all thought they were connected,' I explained. 'But our sick minds went more to a romantic involvement.' That brought a smile to Ash's face. I know, hard to believe, but it had seemed like an explanation at the time. 'Mother and son. Wow!'

'Understatement of the year.'

'Yeah. You could say that.'

I needed to digest this piece of information. Would it change anything? And if it did, what?

Chapter Twenty-Five

Metisse was distant in his love making.

Dread closed like strong fingers around my heart as we lay in bed. My head rested on his shoulder and his arm around me felt good. It felt safe, but that was in stark contrast to the vibes I was getting from Metisse.

I softly stroked his chest, following the contours of his pecs. This always excited him, now he hardly reacted. He stared at my bedroom ceiling. His eyes were wide open, his breathing regular, nothing wrong there. Just the aura that was off. And that—I had learned—was very frightening.

I had to ask him what was wrong, but I didn't dare. I was so scared of what he might say. What he would say. Deep down inside I guess I knew. I'd always known. But I pushed everything to the back of my mind since I found out that my mother might be alive. I couldn't have anymore complications in my life. Not now.

Maybe if I just pretended there was nothing wrong. Maybe it was just something temporary. It could go away.

Yeah, pull the other one. It's got bells on it.

I lifted my upper body onto my elbow and looked at Metisse. He avoided my gaze. Any conviction it might still be okay went out the window.

'Metisse.' He continued to stare at the ceiling.

'Please Metisse, will you look at me?'

He turned and tried a smile. The edges of his lips curled up but it didn't make it to his eyes. There was moisture at the edge of them. He blinked. I think in an attempt to hide the tears. I softly stroked his face. What was so bad?

'What's going on?' I asked him.

He was about to say something when I added; 'and don't say nothing. Because I can see that's not the case.' My own tears pricked at the back of my eyes. The constriction in my throat made talking in a calm voice almost impossible.

'What's wrong?'

He sighed and turned his gaze back to the ceiling, further restricting my breath.

'Everything,' he finally answered in his normal dramatic manner. I let out my breath. At least it was a start.

'Just everything? That's quite a lot,' I tried to lighten the mood a bit. 'Could you be more precise?'

He turned to me again and smiled. This time a real smile. I returned the gesture and momentarily saw the Metisse I know and love so much.

'Okay, everything is maybe a bit much.' That was better. 'It just feels that way.'

Shit, I spoke too soon.

'Spill the beans, Metisse. You're scaring me.'

I pushed my body upright and tucked my legs underneath me as I sat opposite him on the bed covers. Metisse looked at me, then moved up with his back to the headboard. He swallowed and looked at me.

'This whole prophecy thing,' he started. I nodded and urged him on, despite the ice cold pins and needles that slowly made their way up my spine.

'What about the prophecy?'

'It's too weird.' Well, that's something we agree on. Our lives were in a constant state of chaos. Add Alex's revelations to that and weird didn't cover it.

'And too dangerous.'

That surprised me. Sure, we were at war with the Council, so a very real and present danger. But the threat of them always hung over the Sabre's.

'We were relatively safe here,' he continued. 'The Council left us alone.' He conveniently left out the fact the Council sent me to kill him. 'Now we have a target on our backs. There's nothing left of our normal lives. We can't even travel anymore. They know now where we are and who we are.'

'They already knew that.' I answered confused. 'They sent me, remember.'

'Yeah. But now they know for sure. You heard Alex. They know us by name. Our addresses. Alex shared all that with them while you two were chasing us.'

Now that sounded like a real reproach. My patience ran thin as it was, and Metisse blaming me for his perceived misfortunes was not helping any.

'You brought us into the spotlights. After all the centuries we spent creating this place and our identities here; we now have to hide. We can't go about our work anymore. Or anything else.'

'Like your trips abroad?' My anger pushed at the edges of my restraint.

'Yes. Like that. We can't do what we used to.'

'Party?'

'What's wrong with that?'

He was pushing me to become angry, and the worst thing about it all was that he knew. I got the distinct impression he was intentionally baiting me. Trying to get me mad. Well, it was working.

'Everything.' I couldn't help myself. 'How can you be so shallow? Do you really value your parties and privileged life above the freedom this fight could give you, me and all paranormals?'

'I don't care about other paranormals. Let them take care of themselves. I care about my clan. About my mother. My family. My friends.'

It registered that he didn't name me in the list. I felt an almost physical stab in my heart.

'You don't mean that, Metisse.'

'I do. I don't give a shit about your precious Wolves, or the wizards or any of them. I take care of mine.'

'And am I part of that?'

He swallowed audibly and turned his gaze away from me.

He didn't answer.

'What's really going on here, Metisse?' I asked after two minutes of heavy silence. Dread crept up over my whole body and I almost shook with the effort of talking. He wasn't like this. There was something else. A real reason. He was pushing me away.

'What do you mean?' Half-heartedly.

'You're baiting me. Fishing for a fight. Why? What aren't you telling me?'

He looked at me again. His eyes gazed into mine. I saw the pain. Almost touched it. It was a solid entity between us.

'I can't live like this.' I had to strain to hear. The pounding of my heart nearly drowned out his soft whispers.

'Like what?'

His hand encompassed the room, and me. 'This.' I stayed silent. The apprehension paralysed me. 'You, me, Gabriel. I can't take it anymore.'

It was out.

The root of the problem.

'I can't share you, Trish.' His hand came up to softly stroke the side of my face and wipe away the silent tears that wound their way down from my eyes over my cheek to my jawline. 'I tried. But I can't. It's too much. It's killing me.'

I couldn't speak. Words formed in my mind and dissolved on the way to my mouth. What was I supposed to say?

'I love you with all my heart,' he continued. 'But I can never expect that from you. At most; half of yours. No more. It's not enough.'

'But I love you too. With all my heart. Not just half.'

'Yeah. But you love Gabe as well, right.'

'Yes. Both of you.'

'It's not possible. You can't love us both the same. At least one has to be the true love.'

'You both are. You're both my soulmates.'

'That's not enough.'

'It's not a conscious choice, Metisse.' My fear made way for anger again. 'I didn't ask to bond with two of you. I wasn't even looking for one, let alone two. It happened. I can't change that. God knows I wish I could.'

'You could if you really wanted to. You can choose.'

'No.'

'You just don't want to.' He started to shout at me.

Metisse threw back the covers and got out of bed. He stomped to his clothes and started to dress. I just sat there and tried in vain to contain my anger. It pushed at the edge of my restraint. I could feel the fur bristle on my back. A mixture of the tawny and the black. Anger melted them into one.

Then he pushed the knife home. 'And a Wolf to boot.' The trump card. He knew that would make me fuming. I saw it in his face. In the way he hesitated before he spat out what was really the sting to his massive ego.

'That's what it's about?' My voice was dangerously soft and extremely clear. I saw him hesitate. A reflective reaction to the danger emanating from me. He saw the fur pricking through my skin, then retracting, the drops of blood that dripped from my hands to the sheets as I clenched my fists in an attempt to stop the claws from growing.

'That's it?' I asked again. 'This stupid adolescent Wolf-Sabre rivalry that you have?'

He flinched. 'It's not that you have to share me that's getting to you. Just that Gabriel is a Wolf. Is that right?'

'Well, can you blame me?'

Stupid question under the circumstances. It was painfully obvious I did.

'The woman I love, the one I gave up my clan for, ruts with a dog.'

Now he was getting downright mean. Not a good thing to do at this point in time with my ragged nerves and violent disposition.

'I mean,' he continued oblivious to all of the signs and any common sense. 'A Sabre, okay if I had to. But never a Wolf.'

'You still see them as inferior.'

'Yes. They are. In everything.' He spat out his conviction.

'I'm half Wolf,' I reminded him softly. That shut him up. 'What does that make me?'

He deflated. Any bravura he may have had dissipated into thin air. All of a sudden he looked lost. A small boy. Defeated.

'You have to choose.' He tried one last time as he pulled on his boots.

'I told you earlier. I can't choose. I love you both. You're both my soulmates. I won't choose.'

Tears appeared in his eyes as he looked at me one last time. 'Then I will.' He turned and walked to the door.

My anger was immediately replaced with dread and sorrow. This couldn't be happening. 'Metisse, you can't. You know what this will do to you. You can't turn your back on the bond.' I grasped at straws.

'I can try,' he whispered, not looking at me anymore. 'I can't live this way.'

He pulled the door open, stepped over the threshold and took my heart with him.

'Goodbye Trish.'

Chapter Twenty-Six

I was a wreck.

My feelings went from utter depression to anger and back again.

My heart was broken.

It physically felt as though it was crushed into a million pieces, the ache more than real.

I didn't want to get up in the morning, and when I did —because Gabriel pulled me out and forced me to get dressed—I just wanted to get right back under the covers. At night I lay in Gabriel's arms and wept. It must have been so difficult for him. Here I was crying over another man while he consoled me. It was tantamount to his character that he never complained and always held me close. I'm not sure, but I think he was out of sorts that Metisse had gone too. He was not the complete wreck I was, thank goodness. One pathetic bag of hyper emotions was more than enough.

This continued for three days and nights. How Gabriel put up with me, I'll never know.

I had to get myself under control. There was more at stake here than my love life. This was no time for selfishness. There was an army relying on me.

On the fourth day I was up before Gabriel. I spent more than twenty minutes under the shower and let the water cascade over my body. First cold, then piping hot, then cold again. I alternated until every nerve in my body screamed out to me. It almost felt good. Like that one spot that you have between pain and pleasure. I felt invigorated. Ready to take on the world.

Just as well. After all, that was kind of what we were doing.

Our band of warriors was taking on the strongest power in the universe. Not just any old army, but a magical army. The best magicians in the world were on their side.

What we had was dedication and the conviction we were right. That our cause was a just one. We fought not only for ourselves, but for the whole paranormal world, and if truth be told, probably the human one too.

They are theoretically separate; which is the way the Council promotes it. But naturally they are intertwined. We all inhabit the same planet. Maybe not the same space, but definitely the same piece of rock in the universe. That made all of it our business.

There was no room for sentiment. Things were not going as planned. Not even close. I'm not that naive that I expected us to breeze through the revolution. I've seen enough of the Council's power and degradation to know it would be a struggle. Even then, I underestimated it. More than just a bit.

Major.

We took a beating. Not just us. Everyone who tried to join us, or even showed a smidgen of sympathy for our cause. The Council came down on them like a ton of bricks. They took no prisoners. Literally. Whole families disappeared. Others were displayed; their obviously painful deaths formed a clear message to anyone who contemplated joining the Lamaq.

Still they came.

Remnants of once proud clans and packs. Whole families, communities. They flocked to Weisland. We had a chore finding room for them to live. Thankfully a lot of the area around the town itself was wild and inaccessible. It worked in our favour. We could hide.

Such an influx of obviously supernatural talented refugees would make the biggest sceptic in Weisland think twice about the reality of their environment. Even with the forests, it was becoming a stretch to hide the paranormal visitors. Add to that the threat of an all-out attack by the Council and you can understand why we were anxious.

The Council knew where we were. They knew the age old enemies—Sabres and Wolves—were now allies. They knew I was at the head of the rebellion.

Their top assassin was now their number one enemy. They had a point to prove and were going all out to do just that.

Plus, I think Cantix was taking it all quite personally. This was a massive affront to his position. He personally brought me into the fold. Quite a case of bad perception on his part. He had to put it right if he wanted to be remotely credible. If it hadn't been so serious I would have laughed. I really put one over on him.

We had announced ourselves, now we needed to follow up and make sure we carried the momentum forward.

We were the minority. We weren't heavily armed. But we were dedicated. We believed in the cause. I did too. I didn't know exactly what the hell the cause was, but I knew I was on the right track. We had to bring the Council down. No matter what.

Okay, enough of the moral declaration.

It was time to get down to business.

Chapter Twenty-Seven

Our band of merry — or not so merry — warriors were standing around the table looking at the print-outs Alex had delivered. There were blueprints of official buildings and sketches of what he remembered as the actual layout in the lower and more hidden parts of the Council's complexes.

Hide in plain sight. That has always been the paranormal motto. For us, and for everything associated with our world. Now we had to look between the lines. Find what was hidden.

Thank God for Alex. I never thought I would ever be grateful for the geek, but he was proving to be an absolute asset. He knew so much about his—and my—former employers. Things they would be terrified to know he was aware of. Those same things gave us an edge.

I kept his involvement and his history a secret to most of our group. It wouldn't help to let them think we had a former Council spy in our midst. People would just ignore the "former" part. Besides my two beaus, and Ash, no one knew he even existed before he turned up on our doorstep.

Now they thought we had taken a poor dying paranormal in out of pity, or something like that. I left it at that.

Alex was holed up in self-imposed isolation in a room full of computers by day, and stayed in his quarters by night. He didn't socialise. Meals were eaten in solitude.

Most people stayed out of his way, unsure what the cadaverous "melting man," as they called him, would do. They were basically terrified of him, and he liked it that way. He muttered to himself, shuffled through the buildings without acknowledging anyone and was completely weird. Which in itself is quite an achievement in the paranormal world. I mean, we are used to the unusual, but he was of a completely different level.

I didn't want him hurt, and I guess I still had some reservations about his loyalty. Ash assured me he was genuine. His hatred for Cantix overpowered the bad treatment he'd endured from me earlier.

Alex went to Ash every other day for treatment to stop the poison in his veins. The Shaman could only numb the pain and hopefully slow the degeneration of his body. The deep contact he had with Alex's mind let him keep an internal eye on what the former spy was doing.

Never a really trusting person, I had become downright paranoid. Sometimes I thought the whole world was out to get me.

It closer to the truth than is comfortable.

Chapter Twenty-Eight

Gabriel put down the phone and uttered the terrible words. 'There was an attack on the Sabres,' he said, a tremor in his voice.

Ash, Moses and I were stunned.

My brow creased and at the same time my eyes opened to their fullest in shock. Metisse? Charmaine? Were they okay?

'What happened?' Ash voiced what I could not. 'Are they all right?'

Gabriel took a deep breath before he answered. Not a good sign.

He came over to me and took my hands. Dread sent tingles up and down my spine. My stomach felt as though I'd swallowed a brick. No. Please. Let them be okay.

'Metisse and Charmaine have been taken,' Gabriel finally said.

The world opened up beneath my feet and my legs refused to hold me erect anymore. Gabriel caught me before I fell and led me to a chair. He lowered me softly to the seat, knelt in front of me and held me close.

I couldn't focus. Metisse and Charmaine taken? What did that mean? Taken where? How?

Ash joined us and placed his hand on the back of my neck in support. The warmth of his hand on my skin was comforting and I felt calm radiate from his touch. I had no idea what he was doing, but it helped.

Moses handed me a glass of water. I took it thankfully and sipped from the cold liquid. It forced me to concentrate on something else than the terrifying images my mind conjured up.

I sat back in the chair and took a deep breath. The tremors in my hands abated and whatever Ash had done helped me take back control of my mind and body.

'What happened?' I managed to say. My voice had a slight wobble, but it was better than I expected.

Gabe took my hand in his again, I was grateful for the comfort.

'They were in a cabin in the mountains,' he explained, 'when they were attacked by a group of the Council's mercenaries. They killed the guards and took Metisse and Charmaine with them.'

My heart sank. We didn't know if they were okay.

'Are they alive?' Moses asked.

'They don't know. They think so. Charmain's wheel-chair is missing as well. There is no reason to take that if she were no longer alive.'

He had a point. It would be redundant.

'It would make sense to keep them alive,' Ash commented. 'That way they can try to blackmail you.' He squeezed my shoulder again in support.

'If they were gone, I would know,' he added.

I had no idea what he meant with that. How would he know? He just did. I accepted it as the truth, mainly because the opposite was too much to bear.

Ash would never lie to me about something as important as this. Nor would he just say something to ease my pain. If he stated he had that connection, then that was what there was. I believed him. It also gave me a boost. I dared to believe we would be together again soon. If they were alive, we would free them. I squared my shoulders, took a deep breath and looked at my two protectors.

'We will get them back,' I nodded to my own words. 'We need to talk to Alex.'

'I'll go get him.' Moses left the room in search of our mousy computer geek. Once again, I was dependent on Alex.

How's that for a wacky world.

Ten minutes later he returned with Alex in his wake. The small man shuffled into the room, dragging his damaged foot behind him. His face seemed even more askew than the last time I saw him. The pale skin over his cheeks was taunt and in places so thin I imagined I could see the white of the bones beneath. The only thing alive was the fire in his one eye. It burned with an intensity that belied the rest of his body.

Alex was very much alive.

He shuffled up to me and stopped just a metre away. The edge of his lip pulled taunt in an attempt at a sympathetic smile. Moses had filled him in on the situation on their way here.

'Can you help?' I asked with more emotion in my voice than I intended.

'I can try,' he answered without the customary coldness.

I stood in the bathroom. The cold water I'd splashed on

my face was invigorating. The chill porcelain of the sink enhanced the feeling of being here. Something so simple, but so down to earth.

I looked up at my reflection in the mirror.

Frankly, I was disgusted at the pathetic bag of emotions that stared back at me.

This wasn't me.

I didn't do emotions. Not like this.

Control characterised my life. Now all I saw was a wreak. Dark bags under the wet eyes, lanky hair, a flaccid face with downward pulled thin lips. A deplorable weak collection of stupid, needless, and even worse, useless emotions.

It was pathetic.

I was pathetic.

I stood up straight and looked myself in the bright green eyes.

'Get a grip girl,' I berated myself. 'What the fuck are you doing? You're supposed to be the chosen one. The leader of this messed up gang of misfits. And what do you do? You whimper at every turn, every challenge the Council throws up. This is exactly what they want. They're getting into your head. You're dancing to their tune. A puppet to their strings.'

My lips pulled to a thin line. My nostrils flared with disgust. 'Fuck this. You thrive on stress. You're at your best in challenging situations. Stop whining and do something constructive.'

I joined the rest in the meeting room. I strode in with my new found resolve.

'You're back,' Gabriel said, his face a massive smile.

I nodded. 'Hell, yeah.' I answered in a strong voice. 'Now, let's get them back'

It took four agonising hours before we had anything concrete. During that whole time, Alex was glued to the bank of screens in the meeting room. Hastily gathered volunteers filled desks around him and gazed into computer screens trolling the dark paranormal internet as designated by Alex. He was the hub in a massive endeavour to find even the smallest sign of life and a hint of Metisse and Charmaine's location.

'Alex found mention of two high security prisoners,' Ash said, nodding to the wizard.

'There has been a lot of traffic on the dark web. Seems the Council is elated with their latest acquisitions. Lots of congratulations and slaps on the back,' Alex continued.

'Is it them?' I asked.

'Everything points that way,' Alex answered carefully. Then, seeing the resolve in my eyes he added, 'yes, I think it's them.'

'Do you know where they are?'

He shook his head.

'Then we need to find more information.'

'What if it's a trap?' Ash pointed out.

Food for thought. It could be. They could have planted the information in an attempt to lure us into an ill-planned rescue attempt.

Alex cocked his head in thought, then answered. 'I don't think so. It was buried too deep. They still don't know I'm working with you. At least I don't think so. I wouldn't put it past them to try and trap you, but that will probably come later. They don't know I have access to their inside information. If they set it up, it would be more apparent.'

'Yeah, but we don't know, not for sure,' Gabriel said.

'We won't,' I answered. 'Not until we try. We have to

follow our instincts and merge that with the information Alex gathers. Then we mount a rescue operation.'

They nodded.

'There is however something we need to take into account,' I added.

'I've been an assassin for a long time. I can get in and out of tight situations. So can all of you.' Nods again all around. 'What about Charmaine? She can't walk. It's not like we can just get in and free them. We have to plan this. Quickly. Time is of the essence here.'

'We'll need help,' Gabriel stated. 'We need the Sabres.'

I nodded.

That meant facing the clan.

Chapter Twenty-Nine

We were at the Sabre headquarters.

Ash, Gabriel and I stood in front of the massive iron, fortified door and tried in vain to convince the big beefy guard we needed to talk to whoever was in charge. He was adamant that would not happen.

'Mariah said no one outside of the clan.' Okay, that answered one question; who was in charge. It was understandable, she was the second-in-command and now both Charmaine and Metisse were gone, the leadership reverted automatically to her.

'Cut the bullshit, Armand.' My patience was non-existent. 'We need to talk to her now. We can help.'

He looked at me, then at Ash and Gabriel, and finally past us to the Wolves standing by the bikes. He took out his phone and pressed one of the speed dials.

'Trish is here,' he spoke into the phone. 'With the Shaman and some of the Wolves. She says they can help.'

I couldn't hear what was said on the other side, but it obviously worked because he stood aside and let Ash,

Gabriel and me in. The rest stayed where they were, all acutely aware of the tension in the air.

You could cut it with a knife.

I walked through the familiar hallway to the central space in the middle of the octagon shaped building. There were clan members lining the hallway and against the wall of the meeting space. The concern on their faces was mirrored by mine. I hadn't come to terms yet with what was going on. First Metisse walked out of my life, now he and his mother were prisoners of the Council. At least I had some good news to give to Mariah; they were alive. The reference Alex found to two new prisoners who were awarded the maximum attention and security. It had to be them.

We stopped about three metres from the table where the Sabre leadership team was seated. Mariah stood up and looked at me sternly. We had never been on friendly terms and the many clashes we experienced—starting with the one when Metisse introduced me—were foremost in my mind. If she wanted to hurt me, now would be the time and the opportunity. I harboured the hope she would put Metisse's and Charmaine's safety above our petty differences.

'Mariah,' I nodded to her. We didn't shake hands. That wasn't a thing with Sabres anyway. Nods suffice. She nodded back and then looked past me to Gabe and Ash. Again a nod.

'You said you could help,' Mariah got straight to the point. My pent-up breath was released with an internal sigh. Good. We were at least on speaking terms.

'Yes. We can.' I offered the prints Alex had prepared, took the two steps towards the table and gave them to Mariah. 'These are references one of our spies found about new important prisoners. We think they refer to Charmaine and Metisse.'

Just speaking his name out loud cut me to the bone. I couldn't stop myself from wondering if he would still be okay if we hadn't argued? Stupid thoughts. They didn't solve anything.

Mariah took the papers and glanced through them. She concentrated on the ones outlining the security of the prison where the unnamed prisoners had been taken to. After a few minutes that seemed much, much longer, she signalled to Kylian the enforcer. The tall thin man came over and in passing gave me a troubled smile. He'd always been kind, friendly and welcoming, not just to me, but to all of the Wolves. It was good to see a friendly face.

He took the documents, sat down and proceeded to study the information.

'What happened?' I asked Mariah.

She took a deep breath, her eyes narrowed as her brows creased and became more prominent. I saw the slight fuzz of Sabre fur push through the skin of her neck and hands as she forcibly stopped the change. Her anger was mirrored by my own attempts to hold back the beast.

'They were up in the mountain. In the cabin,' she explained. 'Charmaine brought Metisse there in an attempt to make him feel better and maybe even eat.'

Pain shot through me as I pictured my ex-lover in his despair.

'The idiot is battling the bond.' There was a mixture of anger and pain in Mariah's voice.

Surprised, I realised that she wasn't mad at me. Her anger was focussed on Metisse.

'I know we haven't seen eye to eye,' she continued to look directly at me. 'And I doubted your claim to him. But the way he's been acting, and the heartbreak he's experienced makes it obvious there is a bond. And now the moron is trying to ignore it. It can't be done.'

No, It can't.

I thought myself immune to the soul-mate bond. I figured my hybrid nature would absolve me from those tacky details of being a Sabre. Now I had to concede I grossly underrated the pull Metisse had on me. I might be able to live without him, just maybe. But I didn't want to. He was part of my life, like Gabriel. They both were. I missed him. My heart was broken, just like his. Mariah sat down quite abruptly, as though the wind was taken out of her.

'You're his true soulmate. I realise that now. I blame myself for what happened to Metisse. That he broke up with you was very much my doing. I placed doubts in his mind, nurtured his jealousy. Taunted him about sharing you and in the end forced him to choose between you and the Clan. I'm sorry. I shouldn't have done that. I'm not proud of what I did. It drove him to the cabin and now he and Charmaine are missing.'

I was stunned.

Not only by the revelation she'd been behind some of Metisse's doubts, but more because she had actually changed her mind and acknowledged my claim on her friend was valid. I didn't know what to say. I just stood there.

'Can we at least bury the hatchet until we get them back?' she continued. 'After that you can get even, if that's what you want.'

I shook my head. 'I have no interest in getting even, as you put it. There is nothing to get even about,' I added. 'My one and only focus is to get both of them out of the Council's clutches as soon as possible and in good shape. So let's work together.' I glanced to the side where Gabriel stood, he looked relieved.

Ash seemed distracted. His gaze was not on Mariah or me, but to the side where Kylian read through the documents. Ash's concentration confused me. His brow was creased and his upper body inclined towards the seated Sabre. What was he concerned about?

I followed his gaze and nothing stood out at first, then I noticed the drops of sweat that coated Kylian's brow. It wasn't abnormally hot in here, and I couldn't imagine this was a reaction to Mariah's revelations. Besides, Kylian seemed completely engrossed in the papers.

I shrugged it off. There would be an explanation. For now, it wasn't high on the priority list. At least not mine.

Mariah gestured to a chair and I sat down opposite her. Gabriel pulled up another chair and joined us. Ash stayed where he was, observing us all, though mainly Kylian. I'd ask him later what the issue was. They knew each other, were on friendly terms. So what was getting Ash's goat completely eluded me.

'Where do we go from here?' Mariah asked us.

'Let's look at the facts of what happened,' Gabriel offered. 'They might tell us a bit more about the situation.'

We both nodded. Ash also pulled up a chair, turned it around and sat down next to me.

'When exactly did they leave for the cabin and how?' Ash asked.

'Metisse announced he wanted to go to the cabin. Charmaine didn't dare leave him there alone, so she suggested she accompany him. They left Metisse's house on Saturday, three days ago. There were four of them: Charmaine, her guards and Metisse. They took the helicopter. One of the guards flew, Metisse was too lethargic.'

Another deep stab of pain cut my insides.

'Charmaine called to let us know they arrived safely and were installed there. She also mentioned there were a lot of low hanging clouds and that visibility and maybe connections could be off for a few days.'

'She called us a few times a day,' Adrian, the Clan finance guy added. 'To catch up with what was going on here and to let us know they were okay. The connection was pretty bad, especially on Sunday.'

'When we didn't hear from them Monday morning, we put it down to the bad weather. Then Adrian checked the weather forecast and it didn't add up to our expectations. We tried to call but all the phones were out of order. That was weird and we became progressively more anxious.'

Gabriel and I nodded our empathy. I could image they would be going nuts. Not only Metisse, but also Charmaine and her guards were in an extremely remote place. They had taken the helicopter, so no one could go there to check up. I guess on horseback would be the only option left.

'We tried everything, even the satellite phone. Nothing. One did ring, but no one picked it up.' Adrian was clearly worried.

'So we decided to go take a look,' Mariah continued. 'We took the four-wheel drives and went up the mountain.'

'I thought there was no way a vehicle could get up there' I remarked surprised.

'There is, but it's a secret trail. Almost invisible and difficult to navigate.'

Something nagged at the back of my mind but I couldn't put my finger on it. I felt instinctively it was important, but it stayed just out of reach of my consciousness. It would come to me soon.

'We took two cars, with about ten of us. Just in case. We weren't bothered about secrecy at that moment.' Mariah took a very deep breath and I could see the moisture at the edges of her otherwise so hard eyes. 'We saw the smoke before we got to the top.'

Adrian took over. 'The cabin was still smouldering when we got there. It had been torched. Dragon fire.'

Icicles took hold of my heart and slowly squeezed all of the life out of me. Dragons. Like with my mother.

Gabriel put his arm around me to ease the shivers that started to rack my body. The resemblance to that fateful day when I lost her was almost too much to bear, especially as it now concerned more people I loved. I couldn't shake the conviction that—once again—I was the reason loved ones were in the clutches of the Council. I felt my own tears as they slowly made their way down my cheeks.

Ash's gaze was focussed past me. The swirling colours in his eyes were dark and foreboding. I had come to understand that meant he was angry. What could have riled him so much? I turned to follow his gaze. Once again it was focussed on Kylian. I looked back to Ash with a quizzical look. What was going on here?

The rest noticed my distraction, stopped talking, and turned their attention as one to Ash who pushed back his chair and stood up.

Kylian stood with his mobile in his left hand and the papers I'd brought in his right. The sweat on his forehead was more pronounced. His eyes jittered from Ash to me, to Mariah and back to Ash. His nervousness wasn't lost on his chieftain. He looked like a deer in headlights.

'Kylian?' Mariah broke the silence. 'What's going on?'

'Nothing,' he answered very unconvincingly. 'I need to check on something.' He waved the papers and turned to leave.

'You can do that here.' Ash intervened.

'No.' Kylian was adamant as he turned back to us. 'I need to talk to an informant.' Again, that nervous switch of attention between Ash, Mariah and myself.

My instincts raged now as well. Something was very wrong here. I saw the same reaction in Mariah. She stood up from her chair and took a few steps in Kylian's direction. The unintentional step backwards on his part corroborated our growing suspicions.

'Kylian.' Mariah's voice was hard, demanding. It was met by a flash of anger in Kylian's eyes. His upper lip turned up in disdain. A scowl on his face.

Kylian dropped the papers and his right hand moved behind him, his fingers grabbed the hilt of the curved sword he wore in a scabbard on his back.

Ash was already in motion, his long legs made easy work of the short distance between the two men. His right hand grabbed Kylian's arm and wrenched the sword from his grasp. The big man's left hand shot out and made contact with Kylian's head with a massive smack. Kylian staggered but stayed upright. His martial arts background kicked in and he attacked the Shaman with rapid punches to Ash's abdomen and kidneys. Now Ash lurched to the side to parry the blows, not completely successfully. He brought his big arms up and down around Kylian in a massive bear hug, effectively pinning the much smaller man to his body and picked him up off the ground. The air was pushed out of Kylian's lungs, Ash's arms constricted with every exhale. Kylian kicked with all his might but his attempts at escape were without effect.

Ash moved his right hand up Kylian's back and grasped the back of his adversary's head. The blue electrical sparks that surrounded the enforcer's upper body crackled as Ash's physic powers invaded Kylian's mind. He shut down the neurones to Kylian's extremities; the man went limp and ceased all resistance.

Mariah and I were at Ash's side when he slowly lowered the enforcer to the ground. His hand stayed near Kylian's head, the sparks still doing their job. He was effectively paralysed from the shoulders down. He still had control over his face and neck and he frantically tried to free himself from Ash's grip.

Pure hatred shone from his eyes. At me, Mariah and most of all at Ash.

Mariah nodded to one of the Sabres next to her and the woman relieved Kylian of his second sword and checked for any other weapons.

Mariah picked up the phone that had clattered to the floor in the fight. She pushed the last selection and an unfamiliar number came up. In the history she saw the number had been used quite often in the past days. The majority of the calls were before and around the time Charmaine and Metisse travelled to the cabin.

'Who did you phone?' she asked, barely masking her anger.

The pieces were falling into place.

Kylian snarled. The contempt was clear in his face. He didn't look anything like the friendly man I knew and liked.

'Who's number is this?' Mariah turned the phone so he could see the number. There was no name in the contact list linked to the number. Just the ten digits.

The blue crackle intensified and Kylian closed his eyes in obvious agony.

'Who the fuck do you think, you stupid cunt?'

His words were so foreign to what I and the others were used to from Kylian that we were momentarily dumbstruck.

'Restrain him.' Mariah ordered. She turned towards' Kylian. 'You and I are going to talk.'

He spat at her.

Kylian was restrained with tough tie wraps which pinned each hand and ankle to the sturdy chair. His neck was also fixed in place to the high back rest.

He wasn't going anywhere.

Ash let go of his hold and Kylian slowly regained the use of his extremities, though he still wasn't able to shift into his feline form. The process was accompanied by pain and spastic constrictions of the enforcer's muscles.

Between gasps of air, Kylian shot dark glares at us while we positioned ourselves in a semi-circle around the now bound, former enforcer.

Mariah stood opposite the man she'd recently made her second-in-command. Her creased brow showed the dishevel this obvious betrayal brought her. She didn't know how to begin the interrogation.

'Kylian.' She found her voice. 'What the hell is going on?'

He huffed his disdain and looked at her with contempt. 'What the fuck do you think is going on? You dumb bitch. I played you. I played you all.'

What got me most was how he was so proud of what he had done.

'You are all pathetic,' he continued. 'All of you. You think you're so strong. That you actually rule this clan of cowards. All this time I have played you. Pulled on your marionette strings. None of the decisions you made were your own. I have been the de-facto leader of this clan for decades. All you did was dance to my pipes.'

'Yours or the Council's?' Ash asked.

'They are one and the same.'

'How long have you been working for them?' Mariah's voice broke through the silence.

'Always.' His smile was vicious. 'There has never been a time we didn't work together.'

Silence again.

'My goal in life has been to bring this clan under control of its real leader; ME. I am the one and only Sabre capable of leading you and bringing you back to what we should be: the apex predator. You have all fallen into your privileged bullshit existence. You cannot be further away from the Sabre way. You shit on what it means to be a Sabre. You, all of you.' He spat out his words.

'But Charmaine?' Mariah tried.

Kylian's manic laughter filled the room. It sent shivers up my spine. There was madness there.

'Charmaine?' he continued. 'She was the worst. She brought all this upon the clan. She left the way, polluted our people with money and power. Charmaine brought a "new order" where we live among our prey. We hide. You pretend to be human. You renounce your heritage. Sabres were created to rule this world. To be lord and master over all that lives, not to hide from humans and Wolves. You have degraded our race to lowly creatures.'

We were dumbstruck. The venom in Kylian's words was so in contrast to my former opinion of the Sabre enforcer. I berated myself for falling for his deceit. He had fooled me completely. Not only me, everyone. I saw the same shock in all the faces around me.

'Charmaine was my main target,' Kylian boasted. 'When the first attempt misfired, I had to adapt my plans.'

'First attempt? The attack by Cantix?' A vicious smile answered Mariah's questions. But it seemed so unbelievable she had to be sure. 'You set Charmaine up?'

'Of course I did. She had to be taken out of the picture. Her leadership degraded the clan, took us further and further from what we should be. We nearly succeeded. The poison would have killed her if THAT...,' he cocked his head towards Ash, 'hadn't intervened.'

There was pure hatred in the way he referred to the Shaman. Hatred and something more.

'With her out off the picture, the leadership would fall to that imbecile cub of hers. Metisse I could control, easily. He needed little encouragement to make ridiculous choices,' he nodded to me. 'After which no one would take him seriously. Not even you.' He spat at Mariah again.

Kylian turned to me. 'You actually did me a favour. The love-struck idiot acted like the moron he was. Any semblance of sense left him when he left you. It didn't even take much push from me. Mariah did that. All I had to do was whisper here, point there. I played you all. You played into my hand with every stupid action you took. And you had no idea.'

He was right about that, I'd had no idea what-so-ever.

'Charmaine has always been blinded by her stupid useless cub. When they left for the cabin they offered me a chance of a life time.' The manic laugh again. 'I got rid of both of them in one coup. That made me second-in-command. The only one standing in my way was you, you cunt.' He concentrated his attack on Mariah again.

Mariah stood her ground. I had to give her credit for that. She stood there, outwardly emotionless, and waited him out. He was supplying us with more information than he wanted. She expertly goaded him to reveal his "success" as he put it. The manipulator was being played. And now, he was oblivious. He was so caught up in his narcissistic ranting he failed to even contemplate anyone turning the table on him.

His narrative continued.

'The stupid bitch you all are so concerned about even helped me. Charmaine instated me as the enforcer. I alone determined the future of the clan's members.'

'You had no say in the verdicts. All you did was carry out the sentences.'

'Are you sure?' He smiled his vicious grin.

I couldn't understand how we had all been fooled by this man. He was so completely and totally evil. How had he been able to hide his true nature all this time? Not only from me, but from others who had known his for decades, even hundreds of years.

'Any decisions were made based on my facts. On the investigations I carried out. I manipulated the evidence. Showed you what I wanted you all to see. Pushed and coaxed you to verdicts I designed.'

Dread grew in all of us, especially Mariah.

'You condemned innocents to die. All my doing. You took out my staunchest opponents. Anyone I needed out of the picture. You fell for my manipulations hook, line and sinker. I ruled here. I decided on everyone's fate. Not you. You were my puppets.'

He looked so smug I wanted to smash the condescending grin off his evil face. I changed my balance ready to step forward but was restrained by Gabriel's hand on my arm. I turned to look at him. He shook his head, but only just perceptibly. I cocked mine and he nodded in the direction of Ash. The big man had taken a step back, leaving this to the clan. I understood what Gabriel was getting at. This was Sabre business. Not mine. I could argue that I was half Sabre, used to be part of the clan through my bond with Metisse, but one glance at Ash convinced me to back off too. Gabriel and I retreated two steps and left this to those who had lost most.

'My father?' One of the Sabres asked. Kylian's laugh said it all.

'Sarah?' A nod. A broad smile. He enjoyed their pain. Again he focussed on Mariah.

'I poisoned your mind and Metisse's. You were just about ready to jump at the hybrid's throat. That was the plan.' He turned to me. 'She would kill you, I'd kill her in turn and reign supreme over the clan.'

'Reign supreme?' Mariah finally said. 'You're the Council's puppet. They would be the ones calling the shots and you would jump to Cantix's every whim.' Mariah galled him.

'You are wrong. Cantix does not rule me. We are partners in this cause.' His comment was met by general huffs and shaking of heads.

'You are delusional, Kylian, if you think Cantix will let you rule anything. He and Aquanaris do not share power. They subjugate and enslave all. You are not partners. Ha! They did a number on you.'

'You lost,' he tried to bring home a final blow. 'Charmaine and Metisse are at the mercy of the wizards. Cantix and Aquanaris promised me lingering and painful deaths for both of them. You will never find them. This spy of yours is feeding you false information. I win.'

'What part of winning is this exactly?' Philipe backed Mariah. 'You loose Kylian. You and the Council. We will extract any information from you while you squirm in pain. Then we will kill you.'

'I will never tell you anything.'

'Like you have done now?' Mariah commented.

'You can do nothing with what I have said. I wanted you to know who the architect was of your demise. I relish the pain you can inflict. Nothing will force me to help you.'

The smile was now on Mariah's face. 'I wouldn't be so sure of that if I was you.'

For an instant I saw fleeting concern on the prisoner's face, but it was gone before I could be sure.

He spat again. It was becoming a bad habit.

Mariah smiled again, crossed her arms over her chest and nodded her head towards Ash.

Kylian's brow creased in question, then he followed her nod and stared at the Shaman. Fear crept into his face and stature as he was captured by the big man's dark sparkling eyes. There was a distinct menace radiating from Ash. Kylian's breath became quicker and strained.

Mariah smiled one last time, turned from Kylian, pulled a chair up and sat down, ready for what was to come. 'He's all your's, Ash,' she said.

Ash moved closer. He must have looked terrifying to Kylian who tried to make himself as small as possible. He leaned his body as far as possible from the Shaman as Ash walked behind him. Straining at the tie wraps, the traitor lost any semblance of his previous bravura.

Ash moved his hands down on either side of Kylian's head and stopped at the height of his ears. The long fingers spread out over his face and almost met on the bridge of the nose and above the lips. Kylian tried in vain to extricate his head, absolute terror now obvious in his features. Fur bristled in a last attempt to change into his cat. Something Ash did hindered that and the fur retreated as soon as it appeared.

The Shaman's hands closed on Kylian who let out a blood curling scream.

One of many to follow.

Sparks shot off the enforcer's head. There was a distinct smell of burning mixed with urine as Kylian lost control of his bladder. His eyes closed shut in utter agony and moved frantically behind the closed lids. Drool gathered at the side of his open mouth. Blood streamed out of his nose, ears and even from the eye sockets.

I don't know what Ash was doing, but the immense pain was clearly out of this world.

Kylian opened his eyes one last time, the white replaced by bright red blood, the pupils extended to the max. His mouth stayed open in a soundless scream.

Ash continued to invade his mind, attacking everything he saw in his quest for information with a devastating effect I would never have expected from the Shaman.

The absolute terror and horror I saw in Kylian's eyes reminded me I really didn't know my big friend as well as I thought.

Chapter Thirty

'We might have a lead,' Alex stated next day.

Please, I thought. It's time for good news. My nerves were ragged. I'd hardly slept since Metisse and Charmaine were kidnapped. Gabriel had to force me to eat and didn't let me out of his sight until I finished the plate of whatever he put in front of me.

I needed a long hot shower and some TLC. And good news.

Gabriel, Ash, Mariah and I looked up at the lopsided wizard. Despite Ash's help, the poison was slowly progressing through Alex's body. His gait was slower, the left foot dragged over the ground. The blotches of red on his skin were growing over to the right side of his body. I saw angry welts sneak up from his chest into his neck. His left hand hung useless at his side and his face seemed to be even more crooked than last time I saw him.

I felt a pang of sympathy for the man. He didn't deserve this.

'What did you find?' Ash asked.

'There's a lot of action on the Council communication channels about a major strategic success. Most of it is centred around one of the prisons. They mention multiple accomplishments from the past few days. The congratulations started the same day Metisse and Charmaine were taken. I believe it is is all related.'

Alex looked as happy as I think he could be. The normal haughtiness was absent. He was genuinely enthusiastic. His exuberance was contagious and I dared to hope.

Alex placed a bundle of papers on the table between us. There were satellite photos, blueprints and screen prints of messages from WhatsApp and other more inconspicuous services.

He pulled the messages to the foreground and explained what he'd found. The messages were cryptic, as expected. I tried to read between the lines and sure enough, they seemed centred around new captives. There were ecstatic reactions and a general feeling of achievement on the side of the Council. That could only mean they had captured one or more very important adversaries. That had to be Charmaine and Metisse.

We assumed they knew a lot about us; our love triangle, who Metisse was to me, and naturally, the importance of Charmaine to the cause. Only their capture would merit the elation apparent in the communications.

I felt tingles all over my body. My blood raced through my veins and I felt invigorated. My vision cleared and I examined every document carefully. Yes, there a mention of two people. Another about a leader of a Clan, so a Sabre. And finally the conclusive message: a reference to a wheelchair.

'It has to be them,' I remarked. I smiled at Alex and squeezed his shoulder in gratitude. He looked up at my uncharacteristic action, cocked his head, then decided I was sincere and smiled back at me.

'It does look good.' Even the ever careful Gabriel was optimistic.

'So where are they? Do you know?' Ash asked the wizard.

'One of the Council's penitentiaries is located in the forests near the border with Canada about five hundred miles from here. That is where most of the intelligence points to,' Alex answered while he pulled up a google map on an iPad.

'It's an old solid stone building in a very remote part of the forest, in the lee of the mountain. It's completely off the grid. Not officially there, or unofficially for that matter.'

'So how did you get the blueprints?' Ash asked.

'I hacked the Council's database.'

Of course he did.

'What more did you find?'

'Lots. We'll talk about that tomorrow. Now we concentrate on getting your friends out of the mess they're in.'

'How many guards do you expect?' I asked.

'No idea.'

'And the security?'

'Ahhh, there I have more information,' Alex was like a kid in a candy store.

'Because the place is off the grid, it's dependent on an onsite generator. The thing is massive. But… it's ancient. I've seen requisitions for a new one. Looks like they intend to upgrade. For now though, it might give us an advantage. The thing is unreliable. We can expect the place to have faulty security as far as automation goes. That means they will go old school. Guards, maybe dogs, though I doubt that in the middle of a forest. The dogs would have a hay day with all the wild life. That same wild life makes me think movement sensors wouldn't really be viable either.'

'What about magic?'

'There's a chance, but no way we can know beforehand.'

'That's where I come in,' Ash interrupted. I looked at him, raised an eyebrow and cocked my head in question. As usual he just smiled. I knew he could read minds, and after the session with Kylian I wondered what more my big friend had in store for us. I thought back to the earlier conversation about the Elementals. Hmm. There could be a lot more to him than I thought, and I thought big when it came to Ash.

We discussed the plans for another two hours until we had it down to the details.

Gabriel and Mariah gathered the team of twelve people together: Ash, Gabe, Mariah, Alex, Moses, three more Sabres, three other wolves and me. We piled into the three cars and set off for the prison.

Five hundred miles wasn't too far, but that was as the crow flies. It took us more than eight hours to get to the edge of the forest. After that, we estimated it would take at least another three or four hours to reach the prison. That would get us there at about ten in the morning. Not the best time. We decided to look for a secluded spot and get some rest so we could time our mission near twilight. The prison was surrounded by mountains, and the low sun would shield us from view.

As I lay on the bed of pine needles under the truck I had to force myself to relax. It was so double. We had to be quick—rescue them before terrible things happened to them—but to rush in wouldn't help anyone. The tension built in me. Would this delay be the end of my soulmate? Of Charmaine?

Gabriel was on watch duty and I had never felt so alone. It ate away at me and I silently wept for the injustice of their incarceration. I had to get them out of the prison. If, that is, they were actually there. In my solitude under the car, all possible worst case scenarios came to mind. By the time Gabriel came to lie next to me, I was a wreck. Thankfully he didn't ask for explanations, just held me close.

I thought I had imagined every possible scenario.

I was wrong.

Chapter Thirty-One

The tracks were clear in the sand. Wolf tracks.

'A lone wolf?' I asked.

'Werewolf,' Gabriel answered as he investigated the tracks in more detail. The large pads and sharp claws were bigger than a normal wolf's paws. The reach of the steps was more like what I saw with our pack. Okay, so a Werewolf.

'Just the one?'

'Yes.' Gabriel was worried., I heard it in his short answers and saw it in the concentrated way he gathered all the information he could from the paw prints.

He leant over and sniffed the tracks. Looked around for more clues. Gabriel stood up and walked to the bushes where the tracks originated. Here the scent would be stronger. The Wolf would have rubbed up against the leaves of the bushes in passing, or maybe even the bark of the trees. It was unavoidable in the dense undergrowth.

More of the pack joined him in combing out the area.

Ash and I stayed where we were. I watched the pack,

Ash put his hand up to shield his eyes from the sharp sun and scanned the horizon.

Minutes went by. I waited, watched and also listened for any sounds of an ambush. This could be a deliberate action to distract us. Though I didn't expect that. No one knew we were here. At least I didn't think they did. Okay, I sure as hell hoped we were still under the Council's radar.

But a Werewolf, here? On the track, was just too coincidental.

I felt the hair on the back of my neck stand on end. The fur itched to press through, tan cat fur fought with the black of my wolf. The cat was most prevalent. It usually is in tense and dangerous situations. The cat is my best defence. Bigger and stronger than the wolf. It's the best protection in most cases. In this one, it might not be. I would stand out way too much. I pushed both changes back down and forced myself to relax.

Gabriel walked back to Ash and me. The crease in his brow made me uneasy. Gabriel was not easily flustered, but that was exactly what I saw now. That in turn, unsettled me. Ash continued his search.

'It's a Werewolf,' Gabriel explained. Most of the other pack members nodded their assent. 'His scent seems vaguely familiar. I've encountered it before. But I don't know when or where. Must have been a long time ago. Plus there are elements I've never smelled before.'

'A lone wolf?' I asked again.

Gabriel nodded.

Lone Werewolves were an anomaly. Wolves stayed in their pack until they died, if ever. The human-like part of the Werewolf overruled the wolf instincts to banish old and frail pack members because of the danger they could pose to the pack. Werewolves cared for their elders. I guess it helped that they were more or less immortal and "old" was very relevant. Gabriel himself had been around for a couple of hundred years. The First Three probably for thousands.

The only Werewolves that became loners were disposed alphas or wolves that had gone to the animal side; Werewolves who renounced their human side and went feral. Both groups were notoriously dangerous.

This was a complexity we could do without.

Our quest needed secrecy. The shield Ash had placed over us concealed us from magical radar. But other, more physical sightings were something we had to avoid. A lone Werewolf could inadvertently point us out.

Ash stopped his slow turns and concentrated on a ridge on the mountain high up on the right. The trail we were on twisted and turned towards the mountain. He nudged Gabriel who stopped his narrative and stared in the same direction. I followed suite.

There, almost out of sight, even for our keen eyes, stood a lone wolf. The big black wolf was outlined on the ridge in a clearing between massive pine trees. He stood out. Not a normal thing for wolves of any plumage to do.

'It's watching us,' Gabriel voiced what we were all thinking. The Wolf was making a point. It knew we were here and—more unsettling—it knew we were investigating the trail it left behind.

The sun was to the back of the wolf and I couldn't make out any details. The only thing obvious was the size of the beast. It was big. Even by Werewolf standards.

'Anyone know who it is?' I asked completely redundantly. As expected, I was rewarded with the shaking of multiple heads.

The animal sat down on its haunches. It look completely

comfortable in the circumstances. Not something we could echo. What would it do now?

After two very very long minutes it stood up again and made it's way up higher on the ridge. There it stopped again and looked back at us. It waited. Sat down again. Then repeated the action. Stood up and moved a few metres further on what was probably the trail. There it stopped again and observed us.

'He wants us to follow him.' Ash worded what I couldn't.

We all looked at each other. It was the only explanation. But why? And did we follow it?

'What's to lose?' Gabriel remarked.

'Everything?'

He shrugged.

'How do we know he's not setting us up?'

'We don't,' Ash intervened.

No, I thought that was the case. Now what?

They all looked to me for a decision. I had no idea. I'm not familiar with lone wolves. I only know the tales handed down through the generations and that children are warned to stay away—far away— from them.

'I think we should follow it,' Ash rescued me. 'It's the same trail anyway.'

'Okay,' Gabriel chimed in. It did make sense. 'But let's keep our eyes, nose and ears open. I'm not about to trust this animal yet.'

We all agreed and turned back to look at the wolf. It was still there. As though it waited patiently until we come to the conclusion it needed. We took a step forward and the wolf stood up again and continued its track up the mountain.

I had a feeling we were no longer in control of our

quest. It sent shivers up and down my spine. I glanced to Ash. His eyes were stormy. The big man was worried too.

That didn't calm my nerves.

As we made our way up the mountain we were confronted with many junctions in the trail. The very obvious wolf tracks—an anomaly in itself—led us up the mountain every time. I didn't want to acknowledge it out loud, but without the lone wolf's help we would probably have been lost a few times. He was helping us. We just didn't know why.

As we neared the ridge where we saw him first, we got a first glimpse of what was on the other side of the mountain.

Gabriel immediately urged us to stay to the under-growth. There, on the other side of the mountain was a cluster of buildings. We stayed low so our silhouette wasn't visible against the edge of the mountain. It dawned on me the wolf had taken a big risk showing itself to us like it had. It could have been seen from the other side too.

Gabriel, Ash and I crawled up to the edge of the clearing and peered down to the buildings below. There was activity there.

There were four small wood and tent like buildings around a large very old stone construction. It looked as though it had been there for centuries. That struck me as strange. The old civilisations here never built with stone. Not like this. The compound was surrounded by an open space where the trees had been cleared which made it very difficult to approach unseen. The tower like construction at the right side of the stone building compounded that issue. I saw at least one person in the tower; scanning the envi-ronment.

A small river ran between two of the temporary build-ings. It meandered in a natural manner, probably the reason why a community had settled here long ago. That, and the shelter the mountain provided.

The trees all around the compound were dense and dark. A path had been cleared out to one side, I expect for the trucks I saw next to the stone building. There was a junction in the path, one side led to the building, the other to a tarpan on four long poles, that spanned something underneath. I couldn't see what was under the sheet of plastic and moved my gaze to the guards stationed at twenty metre intervals along the inner edge of the ring of structures.

The guards were dressed in the brown garments trimmed with red I recognised from my visits to the Council. That definitely identified the compound as the Council's—and thus; our end point. This was what we were looking for. The large number of guards substantiated our expectation we would find our missing companions here.

Ash tapped me, then Gabriel, on the shoulder and pointed to the trees on the left side of the compound. There, in an open spot between two trees, we saw the lone wolf. It looked up at the ridge and then back to the compound. The animal was low on the forest floor. It made sure it could not be seen from the compound, but was still out in the open for us. A dangerous move. Obviously done to attract our attention and point something out. I didn't see what.

The wolf moved forward between the trees. We lost it for a moment, then Gabriel nodded to one of the tents next to the stream, and there it was. It had managed to traverse the distance without being seen in some way. It glanced up at us again. Then slunk back. Minutes later it was back in the first spot we'd seen it.

The animal was showing us how we could enter the compound.

Understanding flooded into the three of us. The wolf was helping us. He was leading us to our quarry. Showing us how to bridge what now seemed an impossible task.

'There must be some underground source of the stream,' Ash said. Sounded about right. 'The wolf found another entrance and uses it to bypass the clearing.'

'Yes,' Gabriel answered. 'But wouldn't they have thought of that? Put in magical guards?'

That was what troubled me too.

'Possibly, but how does the wolf get through?'

None of us knew. The dilemma was still here. Was the wolf truly helping or was he setting us up for an ambush?

'I guess we will find out very soon,' I commented and moved backwards to follow the tracks down the mountain to the compound. I was stopped by Gabriel's hand on my arm.

'Trish.' There was urgency in his words.

I looked back over the ridge. Two of the guards had pulled the tarp off one of the trucks. In the back I saw the carcas of a moose. One guard got behind the wheel and was joined by a man in a long flowing garb. He was the quintessential wizard. Great, just what we needed.

But it got worse.

The truck made its way up the second path at the junction and stopped before the tarp. There was movement beneath the plastic. Bright red scales on a muscled tail rattled the side of a large iron cage, setting off blue magical sparks. Long claws raked through the bars in an attempt to get at the meat in the back of the truck. The deep bellowing sound of hunger assailed our ears. Even from our perch we almost had to cover our ears.

'I guess that answers the question about security,' Ash whispered.

My blood ran cold as I realised what was in the cage; a dragon.

Sweat broke out on my brow. My claws descended into my hands and fur bristled all over my body.

I had to go. I had to leave. Get away from this totally unexpected danger. A dragon.

The fear of my first encounter so many years ago on that terrible day I lost my mother, resonated to my very core. I felt small, insignificant again. Useless and irrelevant. How could we win if they had a dragon?

Ash slowly took me in his arms and pulled me back from the ridge. His big hand encircled my head as I trembled uncontrollably.

A dragon.

A DRAGON!

I tried to break free. Run. Get the hell out of here.

Ash held on to me, oblivious of the claws and the blood from scratches my attempts at escape caused.

Slowly, agonisingly slowly, I felt a warmth radiate from his hand and enter my head. It brought peace with it. The fear that had taken hold of my mind and pushed the flight reaction to the foreground, diminished.

With every breath I took, Ash's calm took more hold and I stopped fighting him. My claws retracted and I let myself be enveloped by the big man's peace. He placed his second hand flat on my chest. The same calm and warmth that alleviated my mind entered my torso and further compounded the effect. My erratic breathing regulated. I took deep breaths, my eyes still closed tightly shut.

Slowly I regained control over myself.

Reluctant to leave the safety of Ash's peace, I opened my eyes and stared into the kaleidoscope of warm colours in his. I smiled my thanks. He acknowledged with a smile of is own.

'A dragon, huh?' I tried to make light of the situation. Not entirely convincing. But it was a start.

I felt Gabe's hand on my shoulder as Ash let go of me. He squeezed and I turned to him, a silent "sorry" in my eyes. Gabe shook his head. Nothing to be sorry about.

What would I be without my guys?

I'd be a complete slobbering wreck. That's what I'd be. Thank God they were here.

'What do we do about that?' I asked to no one in particular.

They shrugged.

'One positive,' Ash pointed out. 'It's just been fed.'

Good old Ash. Always found a silver lining to everything. He was right though. The dragon had just been fed. That would keep it lethargic for a while.

'How long will that help us?' I asked Ash.

'Twenty four hours at most,' he answered. I didn't even question how he knew. He knows everything.

'They usually eat every two to three days. A meal that substantial will keep him lazy till at least early next morning.'

That was definitely good news. A sleepy dragon was a lot smaller risk that a hungry, hunting one. I liked the odds a bit more.

'We can't use the drones anymore,' Gabe mentioned. 'Not with the dragon.'

Shit. We hoped to use thermal imaging from a high flying drone to determine how many guards there were.

The dragon had superior hearing. It would alert to anything flying over the compound.

'Let's tell the rest,' Gabe moved further back to where the rest of our team was waiting between the trees.

Time to formulate a new plan.

And hope the lone Wolf was truly on our side.

Chapter Thirty-Two

'Do you know who the wolf is?' I asked Ash as we made our way down the mountain following the track the wolf showed us.

He hesitated for a moment. 'I don't recognise him outright.'

'Him?' I picked up. 'You think it's a male?'

Ash nodded. 'His size.' Okay, that explained that. I guess the animal did look quite big.

'You said you don't recognise him outright. What does that mean?'

'He strikes a chord with me, but I can't place him. He seems vaguely familiar.' I was intrigued.

'Who do you think it might be?'

He laughed. 'I don't know Trish. Like I said he's vaguely familiar. Not enough to put a name to him.'

'But you have an idea?' I was pushing. I don't know why. The lone wolf just seemed such an enigma. He interested me.

Ash stopped and looked at me. I gazed up into his

friendly face. 'I don't know enough to say anything. I have met thousands of wolves in my life time. He could be any one of them.' He answered resolutely.

Okay, I wasn't getting more out of him, that was clear. Bummer. Anyway. I was glad the Wolf was here; he was helping us, and we could use whatever help we could get.

Our progress down the hillside was slow. We had to stay under cover of the foliage to make sure we weren't seen. Surprise was one of our assets.

Alex had insisted on joining the mission, and his disability was another reason for the delay. He had trouble keeping up, his bad leg dragging behind him.

He refused help from others, self respect the only thing he had left. We adapted our speed to his possibilities, it was the least we could do. We were here because of him and what he was able to find.

In the back of my mind a nagging voice kept asking whether Alex was really trustworthy. Was he still a spy? Had he been playing us all this time?

I didn't want to believe that. Not when I looked at him. Surely he couldn't still be loyal to the Council after what they had done to him? I pushed the doubts to the back of my mind. He couldn't be a traitor. Not after he unmasked Kylian.

But, I would keep an eye on him, just to make sure.

We reached the foot of the mountain without any disturbance, rested for a moment and took in the sounds and smells of the valley and the compound it housed.

There were no dogs here. Dogs and dragons didn't get along. That didn't mean there were no shapeshifters, no wolves like our pack. That was a possibility, but one we determined was highly unlikely. Wolves were viewed as scum, the dregs of the paranormal world. The Council wouldn't easily employ one, and Werewolves wouldn't chose the kind of abuse they would be subjected to in the Council's employ.

Two of the pack changed, preferring to use their animal form in conflict. I understood that and frankly itched to do the same. But Gabriel, Ash and I'd agreed I would stay in human form, at least for the time being. Smuggling a massive Sabre Tooth into the compound would be a bigger chore than a slender woman.

Besides, a Sabre Tooth's scent might alert the dragon. They had a good sense of smell, along with fantastic eyesight. Wolves roamed these hills, Sabres didn't. Their scent would stand out. The fact the dragon hadn't reacted to the lone wolf's scent was also promising. We were down wind from the massive beast, so maybe it hadn't picked it up yet.

Or, that terrible voice in my head again, the Wolf was setting us up. He was known to the dragon.

Man, when did I get so paranoid? I tried to shrug it off and get back to the reason we were here.

'We split up here.' Gabriel brought me back to the current time and place. As discussed earlier, the team divided into three smaller groups. One went to the right, the second to the left and the group Ash and I were part of followed the tracks of the lone Wolf into the compound.

There was a tunnel of sorts hidden in the dense undergrowth. If we hadn't seen him disappear we would never have been able to find it. It was small, tight for most of the men, a real challenge for Ash.

The damp earth smelled stale and musky, residues of animal scent assailed my sensitive nose.

Wolverines, wolves, bears and badgers, and something I didn't recognise immediately. Then it hit me; beavers. This had been a beaver dam, the river bedding had been changed, either by the beavers or by mankind and left this intricate tunnel and den that was used and extended by many other creatures. Sure enough, the tunnel opened up into a chamber of sorts. Not massive, but big enough for two of us to move parallel to each other.

Water seeped into the chamber from the river and showed how close it was. The musk was more prominent here.

Gabriel continued through the second tunnel that extended from the chamber in the direction of the compound. I set off on all fours after him. This tunnel was slightly bigger, Ash would probably be thankful for that. I'd seen him struggle into the chamber.

I bumped into Gabe's feet. He'd stopped.

We waited for what seemed like a long time, but was probably just minutes. The walls of the tunnel slowly closed in on me in my mind and I was happy when I felt Gabriel move forward again. I peered forward along his body and saw light up ahead.

The compound.

Gabe lay down on the floor of the tunnel and inched forward slowly. He carefully pushed through the undergrowth that obscured the entrance of the tunnel from view. He was wary of alerting anyone in the compound.

I didn't see anyone, but that didn't mean they weren't there. My view was obstructed by the thick foliage that hid us. It worked both ways.

Gabriel moved to the right as soon as he vacated the entrance of the tunnel. He stayed flat on his stomach. I followed his example and moved out into the early evening twilight. The shadows were long and offered additional camouflage for our party.

Ash left the confines of the tunnel and moved to the left, the Sabre behind him did the same. We fanned out into the thick shrubs and made our way forward as far as we dared.

I observed the compound. We'd emerged behind and to the side of one of the big tents. I watched as guards left the tent and walked towards the stone building. Judging by the smells, this was the food tent. Under the edge of the tarp I saw table- and chair legs. None of the chair were occupied. Dinner time had passed.

Moses crept to the back of the tent as the rest of us fanned out further. He would set fire to the canvas and we would use the ensuing panic to move further into the compound where we could attack the guards from multiple sides.

The Wolves and Sabres of the other teams waited downwind to jump into the clearing as soon as fighting started. The presence of the dragon made it impossible to attack from all sides. It would notice our scents and alert the guards. A dragon is worth ten guard dogs. Its senses were much better and its size gave it an advantage of overview.

Gabe and I crawled further to the edge of the vegetation and readied ourselves to jump up and attack.

Shouts and the crackling of fire announced it was time.

The terrifying roar of the dragon broke the silence. It had picked up our scent or heard something. Whatever, it bellowed its territorial anger in mind-blowing roars that turned my blood to ice. I closed my eyes tightly and my muscles froze in terror. I forced my disobedient body to move.

I stood up and rushed two guards who turned towards the commotion of the burning tent. One died, his throat slit by my curved sword, before he hit the ground. The second caught the sharp side of the weapon in his torso on the swing through and went down immediately. I pivoted and attacked another guard three steps away. He turned his machine gun towards me and fired off a blast before the offending weapon clattered to the ground, the severed arm holding it still twitching. I followed up with another slash that took his head off.

Gabriel and the rest were likewise engaged in close combat with the guards that flooded the clearing. From the corner of my eye I saw Wolves race into the frey and Sabres pounce on screaming Council guards. We had the benefit of surprise, but it wouldn't last long so we had to incapacitate as many guards as we could before they regrouped. We had no idea hoe many there were.

Chapter Thirty-Three

The wizard crept forward, uttering strange phrases and waving his right hand through the air. I didn't know what he was trying to do, but it couldn't be any good so I set out after him.

Ten metres from him I was intercepted by two very large guards who stationed themselves between me and the wizard.

Shit.

They were the immediate danger, so I turned my attention to them. One had an ugly looking machete, the other one a piece of wood he found somewhere. He held it in his right hand and tapped the other end in his left. The smile on his face was vicious and full of arrogance. He glanced towards his companion and both grinned. Yeah, well, not a good idea, guys.

I held my own sword and feigned to the left. The guy with the machete rushed forward, swinging the weapon to where my head had just been. His momentum took him further and as I pivoted to the left when he passed me, I brought the sword down and across the back of his legs. The steel bit deep into the tendons and muscles. He sank to the ground, bleeding profusely.

I rolled and slid quickly to the right, under the heavy wooden club that rebound off the ground where I had just been. My slide came to a halt and I turned and kicked off in one movement. I drove into the second guy's space, leaving him no room to swing the club again. The dagger I had in my left hand slide between his ribs and up where it pierced his heart. He went down like a brick wall. I pushed him over, retrieved my knife and turned to survey the battle.

Death and destruction was all around. Most of the bodies were guards, but I saw one of the Wolves lying in a pool of blood.

My heart skipped a beat when I noticed Gabriel's shirt was bright red with arterial blood. I was about to rush over to him when I myself was attacked from the right.

A knife hissed past my face, narrowly missing me. Turning towards the attacker, I ducked in case there was another weapon. The loud crack of the man's neck indicated he was no longer a threat. Ash dropped the body to the floor and winked at me.

I whirled towards Gabe again who had his attacker on the ground minus a head. He smiled at me and a thumbs up indicated it wasn't his blood all over him.

Not everyone had as much luck and I noticed Maraih's left arm hung uselessly by her side. She continued to slash around her with the claws on her right hand. Moses had her back and protected her. Looks like the Wolves and Sabres could work together after all.

Something pushed at the edge of my mind. I couldn't quite put my finger on it, but something was different. Cold shivers ran up and down my spine. It wasn't the fighting or the abundance of death I was surrounded by. I was used to that. Occupational hazard for an assassin. It was something else. I searched the battlefield, what was it?

Then it dawned on me. It wasn't something new. It was something missing.

The dragon. It was silent.

The incessant bellowing of the reptile had been unnerving to say the least, but the absence was terrifying.

I turned towards the cage. The wizard was back on his feet. He stood in front of the dragon who in turn was completely focussed on the man. In the relative silence I heard the wizard utter words that made no sense to me. His voice was strong, belying his wounds that pooled blood at his feet.

Ice ran through my veins.

The man stood upright, his arms spread out and up, his upper back inclined backwards and his legs placed firmly on the ground in front of the cage. He chanted an incantation. Even though I didn't understand the words, the gist was clear.

The dragon watched him intently. Its stare followed each movement the wizards arms made. Smoke billowed from the red monster's nostrils. The muscles in the dragon's legs and long neck tensed and rippled in anticipation. The wings on the his back unfurled as far as the cage would let them. Blue flashes crackled in the air where the beast made contact with the bars. It seemed impervious to any pain, completely focussed on the bleeding man no more than ten metres away.

'NOOOO!' Ash ran past me in the direction of wizard. He grabbed the discarded machete from the ground and thew it at the man. The long wide blade entered the wizard's back below the shoulder blades, smashed directly through the spine and flung the wizard three metres forward from the sheer power of the throw. The man was dead before he hit the ground.

But it was too late.

The wizard had finished his spell.

The words were followed by an enormous bang. It stilled the battle.

Time stood stil as the blue electricity that covered the cage slowly dispersed into the air around it.

No one spoke. No one moved. The silence was total as all eyes were riveted to the cage containing the dragon.

As one, we watched the magic vaporise.

The dragon was mesmerised by what was happening. The red eyes followed the last bolts of magic to the dirt beneath the cage.

I glanced at Ash. His face was grey, the realisation clear what this would mean to the outcome of the battle. The old wizard had changed the face of the battle with his dying words.

My eyes opened to the max as I watched the dragon slowly move its right front leg towards the thick iron bars of the cage. At least it was still locked. But that would be a short respite at most. The big reptile would make short work of the construction.

The twenty centimetre long talons neared the iron bar. The beast looked up at us, and I locked eyes with the creature momentarily. I wanted to move, to run, but my muscles wouldn't work. I stood rooted to the dirt floor, watching my worst nightmare as it readied itself to escape.

The fur on my back burst through the skin in a natural fight reaction. The Sabre was stronger than my human form. But even that wouldn't be anywhere near enough with the mystical creature opposite us.

The talon made a loud metallic screech as it scratched down the metal bar. It hurt my ears. More than that, the implications of the sound were massive and my blood ran cold.

The magic was gone.

...And the dragon knew it.

Chapter Thirty-Four

The ancient animal felt the change in the restraints immediately and acted in sync. With one thrust of it's massive tail it annihilated the iron bars and catapulted them into the stunned fighters.

The dragon was free.

The bars of the cage disintegrated easily now the magical restraints had disappeared.

An uncontrolled dragon was a threat to any and all of us. It would not differentiate between Council and Rebels. It would kill. That was what it was made for. Without direction, it was lethal to all here.

The dragon threw the last vestige of the restraints from its back and roared to the skies, a thick plume of fire shot up as it bellowed a challenge.

It turned back to the battle. To the humans, wizards and shifters. Its prey.

The first napalm blast burned everyone within ten metres of the creature, most of which were guards and wizards battling to re-instate the magical restraints. It was too late. The dragon had found its freedom and wasn't about to let itself be restrained anymore.

It advanced on the battle.

The priorities had changed. Survival now depended on avoiding the beast, never mind other enemies. The massive reptile was the main threat to everyone's life.

From the corner of my eye I saw Ash advance on the creature. He chanted incantations as he moved. Initially, it looked as though there was a positive result, but that hope was trashed when the dragon shook itself and sent another roar our way. It unfold its wings and flapped them. The resulting pressure threw us all off our feet. The dragon towered over us all as it threw us to the ground.

I hit the dirt with a thud that knocked the wind out of me. My head hit the ground when I landed and my vision blurred with the impact.

Through the haze I saw Ash stand up and advance on the towering dragon again. Sharp blue tendrils of raw energy shot from his hands to the dragon. They hit the creature and temporarily pushed it back a step.

Ash advanced again. The intensity and power of the shots deepened as Ash fought to control the massive animal. At first it worked, but I saw the creature sink down to all fours and shake itself free again. It pushed back at the attack, bending its body to the onslaught.

I tried to stand up. The world spun around me. I held my head with my right hand and struggled onto my knees. It didn't help my equilibrium, but I had to do something. I had to help Ash. From the corner of my eye I saw the dragon advance on the Shaman, its head was down low, almost to the ground, and its neck curved. The talons of the front legs rasped on the stones, a harbinger of what was to come.

I tried again.

A hand gripped my right arm. The grasp was firm and strong. I looked up into Alex's face.

'They have to pay.' I heard his words over the roar of the dragon. 'Get them for me.'

I nodded. 'I will.'

Alex let go of my arm and stood up. He threw the cape off his shoulders to the ground and strode to the very unequal battle. The aura surrounding him was bright red. With every step he took, it expanded and became brighter. The magical energy around him crackled and jumped from his form to the edge of the red haze.

Alex neared Ash and lifted his hand in the direction of the dragon. The red energy shot from his form straight to the dragon's head and momentarily stunned the large creature. Alex screamed out his challenge, another red spear knocked the dragon back. Ash regained his balance and added his blue energy to Alex's incessant attack. Together they drove the monster back toward the remnants of the cage.

The beast roared its frustration. It reared on hind legs, opened its wings and curled its neck in preparation of a fire blast. The head curled towards the two puny humans that dared to challenge it. The jaws opened and it took a massive breath ready to burn them to cinder.

I watched in horror as the dragon let loose its devastating magical napalm. Ash and Alex shot their combined magic towards the fireball at the exact same moment.

I—and everyone else—was knocked over in the thermal waves that resulted from the collision of the two massive magical energy blasts.

My whole body screamed with pain as I hit the ground once more.

Everything went black.

Chapter Thirty-Five

I could almost make out the voices through the mist that filled my head. It was difficult and I had to strain to distinguish individual words.

I lay on my side on the floor in what I recognised as the stable-side position from a first aid video I saw somewhere.

I worked slowly up from my feet to my head and catalogued my limbs and the pain radiating from multiple locations in my body. Man, I ached. What the fuck happened? I felt as though a bus hit me head on. Not that I ever experienced that. But it would probably feel something like it did there on the floor. Every cell in my body screamed at me to stay in exactly the same position and barely breath. Anything more than that would be too much.

I complied.

As the haze dissipated I recognised the voices. There were three. The men in my life: Ash, Gabriel and Metisse. They were all alive. All here. A warm happiness descended over me.

'She'll be alright.' Ash reassured the other two. There

was collective sigh of relief. From me too, only I wasn't as convinced as they were. I was the one with the pain, remember.

'I have to tend to the others.' I felt the big man stand up, his hand left my shoulder and I felt a sense of loss. He always made me feel so safe.

Now I was left with my two soulmates. Oh shit. I wasn't up to that. Their incessant bickering and fighting in the past months, and then Metisse leaving, was too much for me now so I decided to ignore them and just pretend to sleep. I fully expected them to blame each other, and after that probably me, for all that happened. They would more than likely just pick up where they left off weeks ago.

I was wrong.

Thankfully.

'Why did you come back for me?' Metisse asked softly. 'With me gone, you would have Trish for yourself. No more sharing.'

I felt Gabriel sit down in front of me. He softly brushed the hair from my face. 'Believe me, I thought about it.'

I could feel him smile. I didn't have to look to see that.

'But she would have been heart-broken.' He sighed. 'God knows why, but she loves you, you pompous arrogant shit.' He let that sink in.

There was surprisingly no reaction from Metisse.

Gabriel continued; 'I couldn't let her go through the pain and loss, not after all that's happened to her. We are her family. You and I. Whether we like it or not. We're all in this together. I won't be the catalyst of her losing a loved one again. And if that means that I have to tolerate you, then so be it. As long as she is happy.'

They both remained silent. I tried to digest what

Gabriel said. He was right about one thing; I did love them both. Equally.

'She was devastated when you left. Physically sick,' he continued.

Okay, that might be pushing it. Though if I'm honest, he was right.

'But she said she was immune to the bond,' Metisse answered surprised.

'Yeah, well it turned out she's not as resistant as she would like to be. Your exit affected her in a major way. She camouflages it well now, but it cuts away at her. Like it does at you.'

'Me? I'm okay'. There he was again, the old Metisse. Waving away anything what could damage his stupid ego.

'Sure, you always have that sickly-grey complexion. Stop kidding yourself, Metisse. You need her as much as you need food and air. We both do. We can't live without her. I don't know why we're in this strange love triangle, but in the end, it doesn't matter. It makes no difference to the fact that Trish is what you and I need in. We can't live without her. And she can't live without us. Both of us. If that means I have to share her. Then that's what will happen. Even if it's with you.'

I felt an immense love for Gabriel. The tough exterior housed one of the most empathic men I'd ever known. He hit the nail on the head. We needed each other.

'We're not so different you know.'

That surprised both me and Metisse. I heard Metisse's sharp intake of breath. Even without a reply, I knew he was as confused as I was.

'Sure, you're feline and I'm canine.' Gabe continued. 'But we're also both people, more or less. Maybe we should concentrate on that part a bit more.'

'Yeah. Maybe.'

'This isn't about us, you know. It's about her. I love her enough to bend. Do you?'

Silence. I opened my eyes a sliver and through my eyelashes I saw my two lovers. Tears sat at the edge of Metisse's eyes as he quietly nodded.

Warmth radiated from my heart to all of my painful muscles and nerve ends.

'Besides. You're growing on me.' Gabriel added with a lopsided grin.

He was rewarded with a reluctant but visible smile from Metisse.

'Thank you.' I understood how much effort that took him. Metisse was finally coming round.

'You're welcome.'

'Does that mean we get along now?'

Their laughter filled me with love.

'You never know.'

'She'd love it if we did, you know.'

'We could try.'

'Not too much though. People will talk.' Laughter again.

I felt myself slip into a soft relaxed sleep.

Life was good.

Chapter Thirty-Six

'Trish...Trish...wake up, love.' The words were far away. Just on the outskirts of my consciousness. I tried to push them away. I was perfectly comfortable wherever I was. The clouds I lay on were soft and fluffy and moved slowly over the beautiful blue sky. I felt weightless, free.

'Come on, Trish. Wake up.' The voice was insistent, pulling me back into the here and now. I resisted, scrunched my brow and turned my face away. On my imaginary cloud I pushed away whoever it was that was trying to wake me. But he didn't budge.

'That's it... nearly there.'

Go away! I thought. In my mind it was a shout. In reality it was silent.

The blue sky around me dissipated and the clouds made way for the smell of grass and earth.

Slowly, as slowly as possible, I opened my eyes to the moonlight.

The first person I saw once my eyes focussed was Metisse. I pushed myself up into his arms and held him tightly around the shoulders and neck. He returned the embrace, pulling me close to his chest. Through the thin material of my clothes I felt his warmth. It hadn't been a dream. The voices I'd heard had been real.

'Metisse,' I whispered. 'You're okay.'

'I'm fine. Especially now.' He hugged me even closer.

'I missed you.' I cried into his chest. 'I missed you so much.'

'I missed you too. I'm sorry Trish. I should never have left you. It was so selfish of me. I was caught up in my own stupid egotistical rut.'

'What about the rest?' I sat up shocked. Realisation flooded into me.

'Alex?'

He shook his head. Alex was dead.

I missed someone else; Gabriel. 'Where's Gabriel?'

'He's gone to find out who's been helping us.' Ash answered.

I looked up at him. Thank God. The Shaman was okay. A bit disheveled and somewhat worse for wear, but we all were. I don't know what I would have done if he was gone. I realised how completely dependent I was on my three men; Ash and my two lovers.

I couldn't believe all three were okay. But it was true. I saw it in Ash's face.

Metisse was back again.

The weight that rested on my heart for the past weeks was lifted and I felt I could breath again.

I slowly extricated myself from Metisse's arms and sat up. An attempt to stand was quickly thwarted when the whole world started to spin in front of me.

'Whoa. Not too quickly.' Ash caught me and brought me back to a sitting position. 'You have to take it one small step at a time. You were blasted heavily. Your equilibrium is still off.'

'No kidding.' I could still see the world turning at a sickeningly fast pace on the inside of my closed eyelids. I concentrated on sound instead of vision, and on touch. The ground beneath me, the earth. I pushed my fingers deep into the grass and felt the dirt beneath. Slowly, very slowly, I managed to stop the hectic images and restore my balance.

'Drink this, Trish.' I felt a cup against my lips. A strange meaty yet oddly bitter oder assailed my nose. Ash tipped the cup on my lips and I took the first sips. I almost spat it out again. There was a reason why bitter and meaty didn't mix. They were the worst combination possible. My taste buds rebelled.

'I know.' Ash held the cup to my mouth and gently restrained me from backing away with his big hand on my back between my shoulders. 'You have to drink it. It will help.'

'It's vile.'

'Yeah, well I ran out of sugar. So this will have to do.'

I looked up into his multicoloured eyes and sighed. Okay. I'd drink it.

'Just don't moan if I throw up all over you.' I had to have the last word.

He laughed. The deep rich laugh I have come to love so much. As usual, it calmed me. Like his eyes. Their effect was a given. I took the cup and drank the obnoxious concoction, forcing it down. It actually got marginally better once I was used to the strange taste.

I closed my eyes again and let the peace come over me. I had no idea what was in the cup, but it sure as hell worked. I felt better already. Metisse and Ash helped me to my feet. I was still a bit woozy and sat down on a big rock.

One step at a time.

My gaze travelled over the scenes before me, from right to left. There was a lot of destruction; buildings and trees annihilated by the magic blasts. Here and there I could see bodies. Their's and ours. Not all of our troops came out unscathed.

Ash patted me on the shoulder. 'You'll be okay. Just don't rush anything.' With that he left my side to go tend to others in need of his medical skills. I was perfectly happy to stay here, on the rock, holding Metisse's hand in mine. I felt like I wouldn't let it go.

'What happened?' I finally asked him. He sat down beside me and put his arm around my waist. The familiar closeness warmed me and I leaned into his chest. It felt soooo good to have him back again.

Chapter Thirty-Seven

From the corner of my eye I saw a small group of people move into the clearing from my right. Gabriel was one of them and he was accompanied by a man I didn't know.

I guessed him to be about six foot, slightly shorter than Gabe, but still quite tall. He wore jeans that looked borrowed, they were loose on his frame. His chest was still bare, the grey hairs the only cover in this cold climate.

One of the Wolves came over and offered him a coat reverently. He accepted and put it on. His build was more wired muscular than athletic like my lover.

He was actually a bit scruffy looking with his untended black hair with grey streaks, I surmised he was a lot older than the others here, though it was always difficult to tell with immortals.

Gabriel and the stranger moved further into the clearing towards Ash and Charmaine.

I watched as Charmaine's eyes opened in shock and her hand shot up to her mouth. Ash mirrored her surprise. He made short work of the ten metres between him and the stranger and engulfed the man in his massive bear hug. I turned to face the spectacle. It was all very unexpected. Sure, I was grateful to the old wolf for assisting us and showing us how to enter the compound unseen, but this welcome was excessive.

'That the lone wolf Gabe told me about?' Metisse asked me.

I shrugged. How would I know? 'I guess,' I answered unconvincingly.

The stranger moved from Ash to Charmaine and hugged her warmly as well.

'Looks like they know each other,' Metisse commented, just as confused as me.'

'You think?' I smiled.

Charmaine extricated herself from the old Wolf and pointed towards Metisse and me. I wasn't sure who she was actually singling out? They all looked at us, big smiles on their faces. Only the stranger was more reserved. He was too far away for me to see his features clearly.

'Does he look familiar?' I asked Metisse. The way his mother reacted to the man made me think Metisse might know him too.

'Not really.' Okay, another dead end. But I'd find out soon enough. The stranger, Ash and Gabe were coming our way.

Gabe's face was one big smile. I cocked my head in question but he just smiled even more. Ash was the same. This was getting progressively weirder by the second. I looked at Metisse who shrugged again. I was getting a strange feeling about all this.

The closer they came, the more butterflies seemed to take flight in my gut. There was something very familiar about the man. But I'd never met him. I knew that for sure.

The way he walked, his stance, everything awoke something deep inside me. Pins and needles ran up my spine and I felt a bit light-headed. Maybe I needed more of Ash's concoction. But deep inside me a voice said what I felt had nothing to do with a possible concussion. This was deeper.

They got to ten metres before I really made out his face in detail.

My eyes opened to the max in shock. I felt all the air leave me in one giant breath. My legs felt like jelly and I thought I would pass out. Metisse put his hand on the small of my back to steady me. I glanced at him and saw his face was lit up with a massive smile, like the others. I looked back at the apparition that slowly approached me with his hands outstretched towards me. I slowly stood up.

The man took my hands in his, the callouses on his palms felt cold against the heat of his fingers. The electricity we exchanged with this first touch cemented the realisation and recognition.

Tears streamed down my face. I couldn't talk.

I looked up at the weathered face. The grey beard unkept and ragged. The hair long and dark with patches of steel grey in places. Deep creases lined his forehead and the edges of his mouth. He had a strong jaw with thin lips that were now curled up in a hesitant smile.

But it was his eyes that held me mesmerised. I lost myself in the depth of the bright green iris' that stared back at me.

Those were my eyes.

'Trish,' Ash whispered softly. His voice warm and full of the love he had for me. 'This is…'

'My father…'

Epilogue

Two days after the battle found me in front of my laptop.

Out of the blue I received a mail from the beyond. Well, not exactly the beyond, but from a dead man. Alex had obviously scheduled a mail to be sent to me after a specific amount of time.

My phone pinged with the familiar notification, so I glanced to see who sent me something. I wasn't expecting anything specific, but who knows.

My heart stopped and my mouth dopped open. Alex? How the hell could I receive a mail from Alex now, two days after his death. With some trepidation I opened Outlook on the phone and looked at the body of the mail. It wasn't much. Just "open the damn attachment." Well, at least it sounded like him.

I dropped what I was doing and moved to my computer. Security was way better on the computer and opening attachments would start off a myriad of extra measures Alex installed before his death. It dawned on me he wanted me to do just that. Go to the computer.

I clicked on the attachment. It was a zip file. I saved it in a new folder and let the security software do its thing.

A few minutes later I was about to check the content when a window automatically opened and I found myself staring at a video of the previously diminutive Wizard.

He surprised me. I sat back and waited for what was to come.

The mp4 started automatically.

'Well, I suppose I'm dead,' he started accurately. 'It was bound to happen. Just a question of time. I hope to God I went with the Council's blood on my hands. That would give me closure. But I expect we're not that far yet. That's why I scheduled this small entertainment.' He looked around at whatever he had set up for this tape and the one working side of his face contorted in what I expect was supposed to be a smile.

'I should thank you, you know?' he continued.

'Not for the way you treated me, not that it was any different than I was used to. No, for what happened after that. You finally—albeit unwillingly—gave me a purpose. A reason for living. Your actions openen my eyes to what my chosen "family" was really about. I spent my whole life in subservience to whoever needed my talents. I was bullied as a child and manipulated and tortured as an adult. The one person keeping this up was me. I guess it was a sick kind of belonging. As long as they tormented me, they at least acknowledged I was there.'

'I don't blame you for sending me back to Cantix and the witch. It was after all, my job. My life at that time. There was no chance I wouldn't return, even though I could easily have gone underground. My rediculous sense of duty and obsessive need to belong sent me into the sadistic arms of my tormentors. It opened my eyes. It finally gave me what I so desperately searched for. A purpose. A goal.'

'And now I'm gone. I expect the endgame has not been achieved yet. We have not vanquished the Council, and Cantix and Aquanarus still have their head connected to their bodies.'

'That's why I'm giving you this. A head start. At the end of this video you'll find my passwords and access to my computers, and to the wealth of information stored on them. It is comprehensively the content of my brain. I have added some plans on how to use the information and even some "manuals". Insurrection for dummies, if you will.' He chuckled at that last comment. Good for him. He was right, compared to him, we were all dummies.

'All I know, or knew, is there. I trust you will keep your promise and bring down the Council. Avenge your family, your friends, and me.'

There in the centre if the screen was the key to Alex's legacy. His astounding knowledge. All his memories.

Our strange melting man was assisting us from the grave. My lips curled up in a smile. This was going to help us immensely. I raised my glass to our strange benefactor.

Way to go, Alex. Way to go.

Next in The Prophecy Series

vinci-books.com/finalstand

**They trusted the prophecy. But even destiny
has its price.**

The war has begun. As the prophesied Sabre-Wolf hybrid, I must
lead the revolution against the Council, but betrayal and a
dangerous obsession threaten to tear my army—and my soulmates
—apart. With time running out, an ancient force rises, and
everything we've fought for hangs in the balance.

This is our final stand.

Turn the page for a free preview…

Final Stand: Chapter One

The war had started in earnest.

Flocks of new recruits found their way to us every day, swelling our numbers to more than three hundred. And that's only the ones who physically came here. There were more, thousands more. All waiting for my sign to start their perilous journey.

Imagine.

Me.

The leader of a rebellion, the size of which had never been seen before in the Council's history.

That's who we were fighting; the Council.

Only the most powerful organisation in the paranormal world. In the human world too, for that matter. Our rag tag army was taking on Cantix; the supreme leader of all things magical.

He was a tyrant. Hated by his minions and subjects. But no one dared go up against him. Not until I came along.

Little old me.

A simple assassin… Or so I thought.

There's a prophecy. One that for decades, centuries possibly, kept people holding out for a better life.

A child of two worlds would liberate the paranormal world from oppression.

And guess what? That child—now adult—is me.

My mother was a sabre shapeshifter, my father a were-wolf. That made me a hybrid, apparently the only one. I walk in both worlds, able to shift into either shape at will. An anomaly, some even say an abomination.

The Council was relentless in its search for the prophe-sied threat to their rule, and I'd been right under their noses all that time. I'd hidden in plain sight, within their own legions.

Cantix and his red dragon killed my mother, or so I thought. I pledged my life to avenge her and to do that, I entered the inner circle of my enemy's stronghold as a master assassin, hoping to get close enough to kill the man himself.

A few years later, I still hadn't had the opportunity and was biding my time when everything went to hell on what should have been a routine assassination mission.

Mixed up in a soul-mate encounter with not one, but two, beaus, I reluctantly found this new vocation; the chosen one. The leader of the rebellion. My single-person revenge became a major war. It was mind boggling.

It was also a headache.

How the hell was I going to lead this lot?

I'm a loner. I don't do well with crowds. I'm not a team player.

'Well, you are now,' was my big friend Ash's steadfast reply. 'You are destined for this, Trish.'

Oh, how I hate that word. "Destined". To me it means trapped, without a say in the matter. Condemned to do what I hate most; rely on others. I know myself, what I can do, what I can't. Others are a big unknown. A possible threat, or at the least a potential weakness.

I know how to kill people. I'm good at it. It almost comes naturally. I guess I should be worried about that, but at the moment it's quite a bonus.

But even that I do that alone, I'm clueless on how to work with others.

Like I said, I don't do teamwork.

And then there's my dad.

The hatred I'd nurtured internally for decades— because he abandoned me and mum so many years ago— was still present. No matter that I'd learned his true motives. My animosity had festered for so long it would take more than a simple "sorry" to change my mind.

That's not fair.

He left us to protect us. A family of three; a sabre, a werewolf and their child, would have painted a massive bullseye on our backs wherever we went. Everyone paranormal knew about the prophecy. Our little family would have stood out like a sore thumb, making it just a matter of time before someone connected the dots and identified us to Cantix.

There were enough who renounced my parent's decisions. Sabres and werewolves have been sworn enemies since the beginning of time. A cat and dog thing, I guess. Always, hereditary, no exceptions. Until they came along and proved beyond a shadow of a doubt that the two species could not only coexist but could also produce what was supposed to free everyone. Me.

And I was taking their paranormal coalition idea a step further. Or a few steps, depending on your point of view.

Not only were my beaus from opposite camps, but the

army we'd amassed featured every kind of paranormal creature conceivable. And they all worked together, bonded in a common cause; to free us all from the tyranny that had enslaved our world for hundreds of years.

It was a noble ambition.

It was also an impossible one.

At least from my perspective.

…Others disagreed.

If Cantix were the only one we were up against—emphasis on the "only" part—then I might believe we had a slim chance of success. But we also had to contend with his mother; Aquanaris. The seer, witch and so much more. She was the foundation of Cantix's strength and power.

I'd only just found out they were related, and I still couldn't comprehend any family bond between the two. She was as motherly and nurturing as a brick wall. And he was, well, he probably made her proud. I've never known a more narcissistic megalomaniac. And believe me, I've seen my share. My enemies might even call me the same, though personally I'm sure I'm in a completely different league to the tyrant.

They rule the paranormal world with an iron fist and unholy magic. Dark magic. The kind that rots your soul, if you have one to start with, and I doubt that in Aquanaris' case.

But I digress.

They frankly scared the shit out of me. And I was committed to bring them down.

Me and my rag-tag army of dreamers.

No pressure, right?

Final Stand: Chapter Two

Even dead dragons have residual magic.

Who knew?

Seems the magic in a dragon is so powerful you can tap into it after the creature has departed this world. And that makes it extremely dangerous.

In the aftermath of the battle with the red dragon that freed Charmaine, Metisse and the others, Ash gathered as much of the beast's remains as he could find. It wasn't without jeopardy. The magic had a will of its own now the host was dead.

We offered to help, but Ash was adamant. It was too dangerous for us.

'How could it be?' Metisse asked with genuine interest on the way back to our compound. 'The dragon is dead.'

Ash turned in the passenger seat to address us. 'I suppose you could say the magic is looking for a new home. A new host. Solitary magic will latch on to anything alive it comes into contact with. That's why we can't leave any here. We need to make sure nothing perilous is left behind.'

'What happens if it does latch on to say, an animal?' Metisse was intrigued.

'That depends on the creature and how much magic is involved, but in general it will drive the new host insane. Controlling magic is difficult and requires enormous strength. Specifically mental and emotional strength.'

A thought crossed my mind. 'Is that what happened to Aquanaris? The magic has taken over?'

Ash nodded.

'Faddon had good intentions, but the human form isn't suited to unbridled magic. He subjected her to excessive sorcery while she was a baby. The magic filled every cell of her body and yearned for more. It's like an addiction. The more she has, the more she will crave. It will never be enough.'

'That explains why she captured so many wizards,' Gabriel added.

'Yes.' Ash's eyes were downcast. 'She steals their magic.'

We were silent.

I felt there was more. Something he wasn't telling us.

Ash looked up and locked eyes with me. He tried to smile but failed miserably.

Taking a deep breath, he reluctantly continued his narrative. 'She didn't stop at wizards.'

I raised an eyebrow.

'Elementals,' he finally answered the unspoken question. 'She captured Elementals and subjected them to unfathomable torture to channel their magic into her own.'

I glanced at Gabriel. His face in the rear-view mirror showed the same concern and pain I felt. This made our quest even more important, and perilous.

'How many?' I laid my hand on Ash's arm in support.

'Too many.'

No one talked.

There was nothing to say.

'Are there any others left, besides you?' Gabriel asked, breaking the loaded silence as the car sped back to our compound.

'A few. Most are in hiding,' the big man answered. 'They fear Aquanaris, as they should. She will drain them of their life source. Their magic. And with each one she not only gains in strength, but she also loses more of her humanity and her mind.'

'Can we contact them? They would be a great asset to the cause,' Metisse suggested enthusiastically.

Ash shook his head vigorously. 'No. They cannot be dragged into this. It's too dangerous. For them and for us.' Ash quickly burst that bubble. 'If Aquanaris captures them, she will become unstoppable. We cannot run that risk. They must remain invisible.'

'But you know where they are?' Metisse pointed out, reluctant to give in so easily.

'Not anymore. I contacted them after I spoke to Alex, told them to disappear and not tell me where they were going. They must remain concealed.' He hesitated then added, 'even from me.'

There was another dimension to his answer.

Aquanaris was our biggest enemy. The one I dreaded most, but silly enough, really looked forward to confronting. I'd always hated her with a passion. The understanding that she was behind everything just compounded my animosity. I'd decided she was the reason my mother was missing. She was the reason for everything terrible I'd endured in my life.

But a voice at the back of my brain warned me not to confront her prematurely. She was a formidable enemy. Cleaver, strong and single-minded, she craved power. Like

Ash said, she had an addiction. One she had no intention of defeating.

He didn't say so, but Ash was definitely in her crosshairs. I may be wrong, but he was the most powerful paranormal I'd ever known and probably ever will, and an elemental to boot. That made him the ultimate prize for a power greedy megalomaniac.

Strategically, I was reluctant to put him in the firing line, he was our greatest asset. Especially now Alex was gone.

Though gone might not be the right word.

His legacy lived on.

Final Stand: Chapter Three

'Alex was a very powerful wizard,' Ash informed us.

The gang was back together around the big table in my cabin. We'd made good time and gathered to discuss the missions and to decompress.

'So how come he couldn't stop Aquanaris from poisoning him?'

'He was powerful, but not to such a degree that he was able to withstand the power of both Aquanaris and Cantix together. He decided he—and the world—would be better off if they thought he was useless and weak. Aquanaris dismissed him easily, thinking him inferior because of his stutter and his appearance. She didn't take a second look at him. If she had, she'd have torn his powers away and increased her own immensely. He chose a long lingering death where he would have the option for revenge over a quicker, potentially even more painful but shorter one.'

Right. Just what I needed, to feel even worse about the little man.

'I still feel guilty about how I treated him,' I admitted.

'Why?' Ash was clearly surprised.

'I should have been fairer. I knew he was a spy, but it doesn't compensate for the pain and hatred I caused.'

'He didn't hate you.'

I stared at him; sure he was kidding me. 'What? Of course he did. He resented me. He said so.'

Ash chuckled. 'He didn't,' he replied. 'He respected you.' He let that sink in before adding, 'but he loved winding you up, and pushing your buttons.'

'The little shit!' I blurted out.

Everyone laughed, including me.

'And you knew?'

Ash shrugged. Yes. He'd known. And he hadn't mentioned it to me. 'I figured he'd earned that.'

I pulled my lips down in mock indignation. 'Thanks for nothing.'

That elicited more laughs all around again.

The mood was lightened. A scarce event in the past months. We needed to relieve the tension, but it was hard. Everyone looked at us to lead them to yet another victory and we were basically winging it.

There was a flip side of our successful mission to free the prisoners. The obvious success was a fantastic boost to morale, and we got Metisse and Charmaine back, but it made people impatient. They wanted to continue our advance. No matter that it had been a surprise attack, and we'd now lost that advantage.

The Council had been shocked. In their arrogance and perceived superiority, they'd never contemplated a defeat, not even such a local—and to be truthful small—one. Still, we'd hit them hard. Liberating important prisoners, not just Charmaine and Metisse, but also wizards and leaders they wanted to keep under their thumb.

Fifty-seven prisoners were incarcerated in the facility we'd attacked. Most of them clan and pack leaders, but also thirteen powerful wizards. They were an unexpected benefit to our cause, swelling our ranks with magical power of our own. Together with Ash, they managed to shield our raids and attacks from the Council, ensuring success. But our advantage would not last for long. The Council was alerted to our additional magical power and was taking counter measures. We had no idea what they were capable of, so we wanted to remain careful.

Our message of restraint wasn't received well by every-one, as we encountered in a meeting of the pack, wizard and clan leaders.

'We need to push forward, make the most of the momentum we have now,' John, the Los Angeles pack Alpha urged. 'Free our brothers and sisters in other prisons.'

The general voice of agreement echoed the sentiment.

'Not yet,' I countered. 'We must be careful. The Council will expect us to attack there. They'll be waiting for us.'

'Let them,' he shouted arrogantly. 'We'll make short work of them.'

I let the cheers die down before I answered. 'We wouldn't.'

Not a popular comment, judging by the dark looks.

'They are still much stronger than us. We had the element of surprise. That's gone now. Another attack on a prison would be pure suicide.'

'For them.'

'For us,' Gabriel interjected loudly, drowning out the disgruntled proclamations. 'Trish is right. We can't be reck-less. That's what they're counting on.'

'But we have more magic of our own now.' John was

reluctant to back down. 'And they've lost the dragon. The last one. That must account for something.'

'It does,' Ash joined in the debate. 'That's why we haven't lost anyone with the other raids up till now.'

'So let's hit the prisons again.'

'Do we even know where they are?' A voice of reason asked from the crowd, effectively silencing the discontent.

'I understand your eagerness,' I continued. 'Too many of you have relatives and friends in the Council's clutches. They are important to us too. We will do everything we can to free them as soon as possible. But it doesn't make sense to recklessly mount an attack without good preparation. We don't know exact locations, that needs further investigation. After the last mission, the Council changed the locations of most of the prisons we knew about. We also need to be sure we're not walking into a trap, or we'll join our loved ones looking out between the bars.'

'We lost a powerful ally in Alex,' I emphasised. 'He was the one who found the prisons to start with.'

'The geeky guy? The melting man.'

I winced. John echoed the sentiment I'd had before, but now it sounded cruel and disrespectful.

'His name was Alex,' I stated clearly, drowning out the murmurs.

'What was wrong with him anyway?' Another asked.

'He crossed Aquanaris.' Ash beat me to it.

That resonated.

'She did that?' John didn't sound so sure of himself anymore.

The big man nodded. 'She did that.'

We let it sink in.

You could have heard a pin drop.

'She killed him slowly, the pain was absolute torture,' Ash explained pushing the message home very graphically.

'Aquanaris is not to be underestimated. And neither is Cantix,' Gabriel added. 'You've seen the result of their anger.'

There were disgruntled murmurs of agreement. No one was happy, but then again, neither were we. The group dispersed slowly, reluctant to leave without their intended results, but scared of the possible outcome.

Our small core team stayed behind in the meeting room.

'They have a point,' Ishmael commented.

'I know,' I answered. 'I'd probably be just as impatient if my friends or family were wasting away in a Council prison.'

I immediately regretted my words. It was about my family as well. We were still looking for my mother. I glanced guiltily at my father, but he just nodded his agreement. He knew how I'd meant it.

'How do we proceed?' Metisse asked. 'Now Alex is gone.'

'We have his legacy. But we need someone, another technical expert, to help the team use what Alex left us.'

'How about Mariah?' Metisse suggested. 'She's something of a computer wizard herself. Maybe she could help.'

'She is very good,' Charmaine validated. 'And I'm sure she'd help. Sitting around is not her thing either. I'll ask her.'

'Thanks. There's a wealth of information in what he left behind, but I really wouldn't know where to start.' The relief was immediate and felt good, maybe we could proceed with the valuable data Alex left behind.

'I can help too,' Ishmael volunteered. 'I've become

rather adept at trolling the dark web and the paranormal one in the past decades.'

Of course, he'd been searching for Embre all this time. It made sense that he'd used the same media.

'Let's make this a priority.' My mood picked up substantially with the options we now had. 'Find out the most current data and work from there.'

There were nods all around and Charmaine, Ishmael and Metisse left to talk to Mariah.

We had an opening.

No matter how small.

Grab your copy...
vinci-books.com/finalstand